REIGN WITH AXE AND SHIELD

REIGN WITH AXE AND SHIELD

METAMORPHOSIS ONLINE™ BOOK THREE

NATALIE GREY

MICHAEL ANDERLE

DISRUPTIVE IMAGINATION

This book is a work of fiction.
All of the characters, organizations, and events portrayed in this novel are either products of the author's imagination or are used fictitiously. Sometimes both.

Copyright © 2019 Natalie Grey and Michael Anderle
Cover copyright © LMBPN Publishing
A Michael Anderle Production

LMBPN Publishing supports the right to free expression and the value of copyright. The purpose of copyright is to encourage writers and artists to produce the creative works that enrich our culture.

The distribution of this book without permission is a theft of the author's intellectual property. If you would like permission to use material from the book (other than for review purposes), please contact support@lmbpn.com. Thank you for your support of the author's rights.

LMBPN Publishing
PMB 196, 2540 South Maryland Pkwy
Las Vegas, NV 89109

First US edition, May 2019
Print ISBN: 978-1-64202-261-2

REIGN WITH AXE AND SHIELD TEAM

Thanks to our JIT Readers

Mary Morris
Jeff Eaton
Nicole Emens
Jeff Goode
Dorothy Lloyd
Larry Omans
Misty Roa
John Ashmore
Kelly O'Donnell

If We've missed anyone, please let us know!

Editor
The Skyhunter Editing Team

From Natalie

For M and T

From Michael

To Family, Friends and
Those Who Love
To Read.
May We All Enjoy Grace
To Live The Life We Are
Called.

CHAPTER ONE

The computer rang and rang, and Gracie jiggled her leg impatiently. Maybe she should hang up. After all, if she didn't hang up—

The call connected with a *bloop* that sent her stomach flip-flopping out of her torso and into some interdimensional abyss. Somewhat unfairly, since her stomach seemed to be entirely gone from this plane of existence, she was also completely sure that she was going to throw up.

That wasn't going to be a great way to start this conversation.

Jay appeared, smiling. "There's the champion," he said.

Gracie had forgotten literally every word she knew.

"Gracie?" Jay leaned forward, frowning at his screen. "I think you froze." She could see a beer in his hand. "I was toasting you. I figured I should have champagne, but beer's what I've got. Aaaaand I don't know if you're even hearing this—"

Gracie finally managed to make a noise come out.

Unfortunately, it was halfway between a braying donkey and a quack, and she choked and started coughing.

"Gracie?" Jay had been inspecting the connection interface, but now his eyes jerked up to the screen. "Are you okay?"

"Sorry." Gracie leaned over, coughing, pounding herself on the chest with her fist. "Sec."

She remembered words again. That was convenient.

She looked up, expecting to see Alex staring at her from around the door, but he was wisely staying hidden. She glared in the direction of his room anyway—this was all his fault—and then looked back at Jay.

Oh, shit. She had to say something.

"Can I, uh—" *Ohshitohshit.* "I need to say something." She wasn't entirely sure she got the syllables in the right order.

"Sure." Jay looked a bit worried now.

Ohshitohshitohshit—

"I really like you." Gracie felt herself go tomato red. What was this, fourth grade? She dropped her face into her hands. "I'm sorry. I don't know how to do this. I'm really sorry. I—"

"Gracie." Jay sounded like he was trying very hard not to laugh. "Why are you apologizing?"

"I don't know!" Gracie waved her hands. "I don't *know.* I'm sorry."

"You're doing it again."

"Yeah, yeah, shut up."

Now a tiny snort of laughter *did* escape him. "So, uh…" He cleared his throat and fell silent.

Gracie hunched her shoulders. She could not look at

him. She did not have that much courage. She'd never had that much courage. Right now, she was frantically sifting through every memory she had of him, trying to figure out if he had ever, by so much as a *word*, indicated he might be into her.

He hadn't. She was fairly sure he hadn't.

So what the hell was she doing? She was blowing up the guild, and—

"Gracie?"

"Yeah?" There ensued a long enough pause that she took a deep breath and looked up at him.

"You're not... I mean, this seems real. Is it?" Jay shook his head. "It doesn't seem like it *could* be real."

"Why not?" Gracie said heatedly. Her pride was pricked, although she wasn't exactly sure why. "Why wouldn't—"

"Well, for one thing, the last thing *I* knew, you were dating casino managers."

"Oh, for the love of God." Gracie threw up her hands. "*One* casino dude. One time. I walked out on him after twenty minutes because he was a giant douche. Otherwise, I don't."

"Date casino managers?"

"Date anyone," Gracie said grumpily. "If you must know." She saw his frown and scowled. "What?"

"How is that *possible*?" Jay asked. "I mean, *look* at you. You're amazing. You look like a model, you're smart, you make me laugh like crazy, and you've got a *filthy* mouth, which is always hilarious. How do you not get asked out all the time?"

"See..." Gracie chewed her lip. "Now I feel like maybe there's something wrong with me you just can't see from that end. Because I don't. *I don't know!* I don't really go out. I mostly hang out with Alex, honestly, and I practiced avoidance when people were at bars when I was working, because, well, casino. So, I don't know." She shrugged. "Look, can we just forget I said anything?"

"No," Jay said blandly.

Gracie felt her stomach twist, and she swallowed.

Then he was laughing. "Do you actually not see what's going on here? Because I'm pretty sure I've been as obvious as fuck about how I feel about you."

Gracie stared at him. Her pulse was beginning to speed, and there was something in her chest that felt very much like a flutter of hope. Or possibly an alien egg pod. Knowing her luck, probably the latter. "Uh…"

"Gracie, I'm crazy about you." Jay had put down the beer. He was shaking his head, laughing. "I thought you were the coolest thing on two feet the first night I met you, and—well, I still thought you were a dude at that point."

Gracie started laughing.

"These past few weeks have been some of the best of my life," Jay told her. "And I got *fired* during that time. I have no business being this happy right now, and the reason I am anyway is because of *you*."

"Well, what about you?" Gracie burst out. *"You're* not dating anyone?"

Jay, who had been taking a sip of beer, gave a snort and a laugh, choked, and bent away to wipe his mouth. He held up a hand. She could still hear him laughing in the background, even as he coughed.

"No," he said finally. "I worked a night shift at a video

game company, almost all of my coworkers were guys, and I look like *this*." He waved his hand at himself.

"You're *crazy*," Gracie said, repeating the gesture mockingly. "You have *a complex*." Another hand wave. "You're a *perfectly good-looking guy*."

"All this mockery from the woman who apologized three times for telling me she liked me and then tried to hang up the call?" Jay asked pointedly.

Gracie scowled at him.

Jay cleared his throat. "I think we're getting off-track."

"Right." Gracie sandwiched her hands between her knees and wrinkled her nose. "What were we talking about?"

"The fact that we like each other, woman."

"Oh. Yeah." Despite herself, she felt a grin spreading across her face. "Really?"

Jay was laughing hysterically at this point. "Yes," he managed. "Really. Good Lord! How you could think for a *second* that I wasn't into you is beyond me."

"Yeah, well, it's never obvious to the people involved. How could *you* not think *I* was into *you*?" Gracie crossed her arms and raised an eyebrow. "I was pretty obvious."

"I couldn't tell!" Jay waved his hands, got beer all over the wall, and stared at it for a moment before putting his bottle down. "I'm going to leave this here. Look, you were nice to *everyone*."

"Oh, for—" Gracie groaned. Then, despite herself, she yawned. "Oh, God, now that I'm not nervous as fuck, I'm so tired."

"Well, it's been a long night," Jay pointed out. "What with beating the quest and all. And we were on a hair trigger, ready to drop in and just go as soon as we got the okay." He yawned as well. "Now you've got me yawning, too. Dammit."

"Sorry. And that *was* tonight, wasn't it? Huh." Gracie tucked a lock of hair behind her ear and yawned again. She couldn't keep her eyes open all of a sudden. "This is embarrassing; I'm so sorry. I drop this on you and then—"

"Gracie, get some *sleep*. We'll talk about this more tomorrow, okay? I'll be here. Whenever." When she looked up, his eyes were tracing her face as if he'd never seen her before, he had a half-smile playing around his lips, and his brown eyes were very warm.

"Okay." Gracie grinned at him. "You get some sleep, too."

"You think I could sleep after that?" He gave a little laugh. "I want to go yell from the rooftops."

"Yell what?"

"I haven't decided. Just yell, mainly."

"Hope it's happy yelling." Gracie smiled. "I'll talk to you tomorrow. I, uh—I don't know what to say. I was so sure I was going to torpedo everything, but I couldn't keep from saying it anymore."

"I'm glad you said it," Jay admitted. "I…was too much of a coward, apparently. Not great for my ego."

"I think everyone is," Gracie said after thinking about it for a moment, "and the people who 'play it cool' are just better at making it look like a play instead of being scared shitless."

Jay snorted. "That makes me feel a *little* better, thank you. Go to sleep. I'll be here when you wake up. Promise."

Gracie smiled. She reached out to touch the screen,

realized that was ridiculous, and blushed a fiery red. She waved awkwardly. "I'll see you tomorrow. Bye."

"Bye." He took another sip of his beer.

There was silence. Gracie stared at the call interface, wondering why everything in the room looked the same when everything was quite clearly completely different now. She pressed her hands between her knees and blew out a long breath.

Now that she'd hung up, it didn't seem real. Had she actually admitted her feelings to him? Had he actually seemed into her?

What if he was lying?

"Oh, for God's sake, Gracie," she muttered to herself. She'd never had time for relationship nonsense, even her own. Jay was a reasonable, straight-talking kind of guy. It would have been clear if he'd been unpleasantly surprised by the revelation.

A small noise caught her attention, and her head whipped around to glare at the hallway. No more noises, and yet—

Gracie slid off the couch as silently as she could and crawled toward the hallway. She had her eyes focused on Alex's door. Was it just her, or was it cracked open? As she watched, she saw it open a bit more.

She had one chance to pull this off. Gracie scrambled to get over next to the door as quietly as she could, and when Alex finally stuck his head around the door…she was right there, staring at him.

"JESUS FUCKING CHRIST!" He jumped and then ducked while Gracie doubled over with a hand over her stomach, laughing hysterically. "Jesus. Holy shit. You *demon*."

"I-I..." Now that Gracie had started laughing, she couldn't stop. All the adrenaline that had built up in her system was pouring out of her in the form of laughter. "I—Oh, God, it hurts."

"Good! You deserve that!"

"Oh, c'mon. Oh, God...ow." She slumped against the wall. "You were...spying on me."

"I was *checking* on you." Alex had picked himself up, and now he brushed off his sleeves with a glare. "To make sure you were all right."

"Youuuuu were snooping." Gracie mock-glared, then grinned. "That was fun."

There was a long pause.

"What?" Gracie asked finally.

"*WELL?*" Alex waved his hands wordlessly.

"Ohhhh. Right." Gracie remembered Jay with a jolt. She thought seriously about letting Alex wonder, but as soon as she thought of Jay, her face split into an involuntary grin. It was obvious how everything had gone.

"Ha! I *knew* it." Alex pulled her close for a hug. "I *knew* he was into you."

"You *knew?*" Gracie pushed him away. "You knew, and you let me walk into it blind? You bastard!"

"You gotta do it for yourself!" Alex replied, holding up his arms to fend off blows. "Don't...don't go all Callista on me."

Gracie snickered. "You're lucky I don't have a giant sword. But seriously, man, come on. You couldn't have paved the way a bit?"

"Nope." Alex was surprisingly adamant. He looped an arm around her shoulders and drew her out into the main room. "It's like this, you see: when you gave Sydney my number, she and I didn't have anything going on, right? You were trying to get me out of my shell, so it made sense to shove a bit. But with you and Jay...you knew each other. What was happening was about the two of you, specifically. I couldn't be the one to do the legwork."

"Did that actually make sense, or am I sleep-deprived as fuck?" Gracie asked philosophically.

"*Por que no los dos?*" Alex returned with a grin. He reached over to shut her laptop. "Seriously, I'm glad I was right about how he feels." He reached out to steady her as she swayed. "Whoa, hey! Maybe you should get some sleep?" He yawned hugely. "I know I should."

"I'll be along soon." But Gracie was looking at the VR suit.

"Gracie..."

"I'm a grown-ass adult." Gracie gave him a grin. "You go get some sleep. I promise I'll sleep soon. I just want to see it all again. The starting zone."

Alex must have understood, because he gave a small nod and disappeared, still smiling.

Gracie pulled on her VR suit. Exhaustion was dragging at her, but the weeks of fury and fear were suddenly gone, and she felt so light that she wondered if she might float away. She'd spoken to Jay. She'd led her team through the quest, and she hadn't fallen to Harry's last, insane challenge.

Of *course*, he would claim she should fight him alone— as if a single player versus a boss was any sort of fair fight.

But Harry was the sort of person who thought the world owed it to him to bow down.

Gracie settled the headset over her eyes and took a moment to bask in the blue ether of the log-in screen before hitting the button that would send her into the world. The walls of the inn had barely materialized around her before she had her character striding out into the near-deserted streets.

It was midnight in the game world, and so the various shops, which were there for color alone—farmers' carts, street food vendors—were all shuttered and silent. Very few people were around, and most of them, Gracie guessed, were idle.

Only a few heads turned to watch the woman with the glowing 1 above her head.

It was a quick walk out of Kithara and into the starting zone, where a dirt road climbed gently through fields of tall grass. Gracie walked with a smile as the sped-up server time turned the deep blues of night into golds and reds. Birds were chirping, wind rustled in the grass, and she held out a hand to brush it through the grass.

If she closed her eyes, she could imagine she felt it sweeping against her palm.

She opened her eyes again and stared at the lightening sky. This was her world—a world she belonged in. A world where instead of engagement parties and awkward dinner-dates, she had friends backing her up, jokes about magic, and a fight for something worthwhile.

She looked over her shoulder, back at Kithara and went still.

Two characters were standing there, watching her: an

Aosi male, a summoner with greenish-blue skin and jet black hair, and a human man, tall and slim, with deep brown skin and a hooked nose.

Gracie sighed.

"So…is one of you Dan, and the other Dhruv?" she asked. "Or are you both Harry and this is some new mindfuck?"

CHAPTER TWO

THE FORGOTTEN KING RETURNS.
Rage. Absolute rage.

For a long moment, Harry could think of nothing at all except his blinding fury. He could not speak, and he was hardly aware of his body or the world around him.

Then it resolved enough to make him want to smash everything in the immediate vicinity.

He didn't. Barely. He ripped the headset off and used every ounce of self-control he had not to scream his fury. He sank into a crouch, fingers rigid, clenched on air. This wasn't happening; it couldn't be happening. Disbelief followed quickly on the heels of anger.

Harry's mind retreated from the reality of it almost quicker than he could chase it. This wasn't happening. It was a daydream, and a bad one—a waking nightmare. It wasn't real, because it *couldn't* be real. Who could have known to take that first quest?

No one.

None of them *deserved* it. None of them cared enough

to save pixels. They didn't think there was any reason to expend their energy being polite to computers. This had been going on for decades, becoming increasingly clear in recent years, and it terrified Harry. He had listened to the things people laughed about doing in simulators, the things they taught one another to do.

They spread cruelty. They learned it from each other, and they spread it into the world.

Because it was never *just* computers they hurt, it was each other. The cruelty sickened them. It sank into their minds and tinged them with darkness until they could not help but hurt and twist others.

Harry had built himself into the game for exactly that reason. People *needed* a guiding influence. And, because he was the only one who could see what was going on, they needed *him* to be that leader.

They could hate him if they wanted. He had expected it; almost, he welcomed it. He had seen from the start that they might try to rise up against him and unite to bring down a common foe. Inspire one another to feats of courage and selflessness.

He didn't fear that. The bonds between them would stretch into the real world as well.

Writing Yesuan's story had been bittersweet. When others had heard it, they were not yet willing to step past their initial disbelief and try to understand Yesuan's struggle.

So it had to be Harry who led them.

He just thought he'd have had more time, but the others had been far too clever at keeping him out of the game as a player. Dan and Dhruv were many things, but stupid was not one of them. They had successfully prohibited Harry from setting up an account. How, exactly, they had tracked him, he wasn't sure. It wasn't his name, because he'd used fake ones. It wasn't his IP address, because he logged on from different locations. He couldn't think of any way it could be embedded in his VR suit, but he'd even purchased another one of those.

It still hadn't worked.

They hadn't closed off all of the game, however. They could hardly manage *that* when he knew the workings of it so intimately. He'd been poking around, trying to find how they'd set their ban so he could undo it when he saw that someone had begun his quest.

Callista.

The name made him want to yell. He had been so damned stupid—that was the worst part. He hadn't thought to fear her at first. He had watched her progress, even spoken to her from behind the masks of the bosses he'd constructed.

Part of him, he knew now, was simply grateful to have found someone else who saw the game world as he did. Someone else who was willing to extend courtesy and kindness to *everyone*. She loved *Metamorphosis Online*. He'd observed the way she lingered when she examined little details of the game, and how she spoke to her team.

He hadn't ever expected her to win, so he'd let the whole thing go on far longer than it should have. Like a fool, he'd *enjoyed* the way she challenged him.

In the end, of course, she'd been like all the rest: grasping for power that wasn't hers to chase after God only knew what sort of goals. She didn't understand what needed to be done, and when he'd tried to explain it to her, she'd defied him.

Her. A nothing of a person. Barely graduated from college. A *blackjack dealer,* for God's sake. What the hell did she think she knew about the world or about the game?

It was supposed to be *him.*

Harry stripped the VR suit off, hardly caring when he felt fabric tear and snag on his clothing. He left it in a heap on the floor when he left the unadorned second bedroom of his house in semi-rural Washington.

He'd gone to Las Vegas to find Callista, and when he met her and realized she would never be his ally, he'd had nowhere to go back to. He might as well go somewhere no one could track him. All he needed was the internet. The cost of living hardly mattered after the buyout Dan and Dhruv had forced on him.

His cabin was surrounded by trees, the sky often cloudy, and the sound of the birds constant. He still wasn't used to that…or the utter silence at night. No cars passing, no people walking outside.

He stood in the tiny living space and swept his eyes over the boxes he hadn't yet bothered to unpack. There had been no time for that; he'd planned his drive here in tiny hops, always close to high-speed internet, always ready to jump into the game if he needed to do so.

But in the end, even though he'd been there and waiting, it hadn't been enough.

He wasn't made for real-time strategy, he thought sullenly. He specialized in thinking ahead. In understanding how people would interact on a grand scale. How they would strengthen or warp one another's characters.

This imposter, this usurper, was a good strategist one-on-one, even if she was a coward.

She should have fought him. If she believed she was meant to hold the throne, she should have been willing to fight him. Honor had demanded it. Who was she to come after him with a whole team at her back and then claim she had a right to rule? Who was she to taunt him that she had a team with her and he did not have one with him?

A ruler should be alone. She could not rule if she was not willing to do so without a team behind her.

Of course, he had always believed, somewhere inside himself, that Dan and Dhruv would be there with him. That they would come around and see that he was right. He'd really believed that.

Perhaps it could still happen.

Harry hesitated, then opened the door and went out into the dark night. An owl's hoot nearby made his heart leap. He still wasn't used to the wildlife. He'd seen deer not too long ago and was glad of it…and then he saw a pack of coyotes the next day, and was viscerally reminded of how little nature cared for his survival.

It didn't matter that he was the only one who understood human nature, who understood what humanity needed in this new era. A coyote would tear his throat out without thinking twice—or thinking at all.

Perhaps that was the problem, he mused. His mind drifted to the opening scenes of one of his favorite science fiction novels, to the *Gom Jabbar*. The Bene Gesserit had known that not all who looked human *were* human. Some were animals, never rising above their base desires.

He was asking too much of them.

Harry took a deep breath of the night air and tried to calm himself. He had *known* they were going to rise against him, he told himself. People did not like being ruled, even when it was for their own good. He had known they would fight him. This would not be the only challenge he faced.

He was smarter than this upstart, and he certainly knew more about *Metamorphosis Online*. While she did this out of some misplaced desire to give people choices, he understood the way the world truly was.

He would win in the end.

After a moment's hesitation, he stepped off his porch and into the grass around his house. Claws and teeth aside, most wildlife wasn't going to try their chances with a human. This was a time when facts and logic went against primal instinct, and Harry was not going to let the dregs of his animal brain hold him back.

He made his way through the trees, eyes adjusting to the darkness, and steeled himself to look inward.

Thinking of his eventual triumph hadn't calmed him, and he knew why.

He just didn't want to think about it.

But this was his *Gom Jabbar*, and he was not going to flinch. He was going to face the truth: he could not do this alone. He needed others to support him. What Callista had said was true in its own way, even if she didn't understand.

That last thought made him stop in his tracks. Yes. Callista had spoken the truth, even though she did not understand. That was the key. She believed that a team of knowing allies was the only way to win. She believed in leading from the front, in being an ideal.

Harry knew better. He did not intend to let his allies

understand his true aims. Some, perhaps, might not even know they were on his team.

Yes.

He turned around and headed back to the house. All it had taken was a few moments in the peace of the outdoors, and he was already refreshed, filled with purpose. In the city, surrounded by people living their meaningless lives, he would have been distracted by their petty concerns. Coming here had been the correct choice.

In the house, he left the door open to catch the sounds of the forest at night and pulled a pad of paper out of one of the boxes. Even when he'd worked all day on programming, his desk had been littered with pieces of paper. He planned best in ink.

It was not long until he had a full list of potential allies, both knowing and unknowing.

His confidence was restored. It was the nature of kingship that people would attempt to overthrow you. That was something Callista would find out soon enough. This had simply been his first test, and he fully intended to pass it.

After all, if he could not rule, if he could not ensure that this game was a force for good, there was only one choice left.

To destroy it.

CHAPTER THREE

The dark-haired human nodded to Gracie. "I'm Dhruv."

Where the air above his head should indicate a name, there was nothing. His skin was a deep brown, and he wore the leather armor of a low-level melee fighter.

"And I'm Dan," said the Aosi summoner. Unlike most male characters in the game, he wore his hair long, and it blew in a magical breeze.

Gracie had to admit, she'd love a world where long hair always blew around glamorously while somehow never getting in the way. She'd bet it didn't tangle, either. Real life really needed to step up its game.

She sighed. "Well, I suppose I can appreciate you showing up here instead of at my apartment." She blinked and considered. "Actually, I *don't* like this any better."

Dan said nothing but she thought she heard a snicker from Dhruv. She got the sense that he preferred blunt honesty and a screaming fight to carefully-chosen words.

"Why are you here?" Gracie asked them flatly.

They looked at one another for a moment, and she had the sense they might be speaking on a private channel. When they looked back, it was Dhruv who spoke first.

"To meet you," he said. Behind the minimal voice filters of a human character, his tone was quite brusque. "You're a fixture of the game now whether we like it or not."

The Aosi looked at him sharply, then back at Gracie. "What he means is—" Dan started to say.

"No, I get what he means," Gracie shot back. "He means you two *don't* like that I'm a fixture of the game. And, like him, I would much rather we just said what we meant—because, frankly? It's been too long with you two sneaking around and doing things behind my back when I goddamned *tried* to make things right from the get-go. *You're* the ones who turned this into a battle, not me."

For a very long moment, neither of them said anything. At least, they didn't say anything to her. What they might be saying to one another, she didn't know. They stared each other down through the tall grass, Gracie's golden armor shining, the Aosi's hair blowing in the imaginary wind, heroes and villains in some sort of cinematic showdown.

It was enough to make her wonder if every showdown was this way. When generals met on a battlefield with their armies behind them, did they feel swelling, epic camaraderie and purpose, or did they feel this utter annoyance that the other side couldn't just behave reasonably?

She was beginning to think it was the latter.

"So?" she said, finally. "Anything to say?"

"We prioritized the game over you," Dan said finally.

"We have spent over a decade creating *Metamorphosis Online*. Thousands of people play it—"

"Yeah, I get that." Gracie couldn't keep the bitterness out of her voice. "I really, really do. Which is why I tried to fix it from the start. You *had* options—"

Dan cut her off with a small gesture, one green-blue hand moving slightly. "This isn't about that anymore."

"Oh?" It was a pity they couldn't see her expression because she was pretty sure her eyebrows had shot off her face entirely.

"This is about moving forward," Dan said. From the way he spoke, she guessed he was used to being very businesslike and crisp. Unfortunately, his voice now sounded echoey due to the Aosi voice filters. "This is about what we do in the future."

In Gracie's opinion, that was awfully convenient. After someone trampled all over you, it was certainly more advantageous to *them* to say that you shouldn't focus on all the bad things they'd done. That you should just move on and focus on the future.

Some quiet part of her, though, wanted to see what they would say if they thought she was agreeable. She wanted to know where their heads were, after all.

Because she intended to drive a very hard bargain.

So she crossed her arms and waited. She didn't quite have it in her to simper.

Dhruv, however, had her number. "What do *you* want?" he asked her bluntly.

I want to be able to play the damned game in peace. I want to be able to have a place where my friends and I can meet and help one another and feel a little bit like the world is a nice place.

She wasn't going to say that, of course. And, as she tried to figure out what she *would* say, inspiration came to her in a flash.

"I want you to keep Harry off my back, for one thing."

She was pretty sure that was the last condition they wanted her to put on things. For another, she was sure they would actually try. It meshed with their own goals, after all. They didn't want Harry in the game any more than she did. They certainly didn't want the ghost of corporate blunders past to come around and harass their players.

She felt—as much as one could feel something like that —Dan's desire to say she could have given the quest back to Harry. But he wouldn't want Harry to be where she was standing now, and they both knew it.

He wisely kept his mouth shut.

That was when she realized it: they didn't want to be here, either. They had no idea what they were doing. They weren't masterminds, running the whole game like puppet masters. Instead, they were scrambling to keep up with a situation that had blindsided them.

She wasn't as out of her depth as she'd thought.

"As you'll have noticed," Dhruv said, "Harry isn't exactly easily controlled."

"Yeah, well," Gracie shot back, "that's the bargain you took on when you started a company with him, isn't it?"

"Are you holding us responsible for his behavior?" Dhruv was shifting angrily.

"You're the ones who helped make him who he was," Gracie snapped. "I know the stories you tell yourself. You say that *Metamorphosis Online* was his idea, but *you* two built it, don't you? You say that. Well, if he couldn't have made it without you, then you had a hand in giving him that power. I'll bet he used some of *your* code to work himself into the game."

There was ringing, icy silence. She was fairly sure they weren't talking to each other. She could practically feel the fury rippling off them in waves.

"Harry's choices," Dhruv said finally, "are his own. You would say the same if we blamed you for what he's done."

"Mmm." Gracie smiled. Anger warmed her, heating her blood. "If you really believed that, you'd have been open with everyone about what was happening. You would have issued a press release about how Harry was interfering in the game. You would have told your sponsored teams what was happening. But you didn't."

Dan and Dhruv looked at each other now. They *were* talking, she could tell.

"I tried to help," Gracie said again. She couldn't get past this part, no matter how she tried. "I sent you a message as soon as I got into the Top 10. I *said* it was a mistake."

"So you *do* think it was a mistake," Dan said quietly, and she had the sense that she'd stepped unknowingly into a trap.

"Not anymore," she told him simply. "Now I know it was part of the game's rules, because it was. I did quests no one else did, and I fought bosses no one else fought. I made a gesture no one else made to end a war between two non-playing races. And I don't think—"

She bit off the words.

"You don't think what?" Dan asked silkily.

Gracie gave him an unfriendly look and wished he

could somehow see it. He couldn't, of course. He just saw the blank, distant expression of her Aosi avatar.

"I may not agree with everything Harry believes," Gracie said, "but I don't disagree with all of it either."

"You should." Now Dhruv sounded angry. "He wants to be a dictator. He wants to hold people back from things they *need* to be allowed to do."

"Oh, come on." Gracie rolled her eyes. "There weren't video games until a couple of decades ago. If people *needed* to be able to do this, the human race wouldn't have survived without it."

Dhruv made an inarticulate noise of anger.

"I'm not saying there should be a dictator," Gracie told him fiercely. "Harry didn't think of anyone else as real people. When it came down to it, there was a reason he didn't have anyone fighting with him. He'd never have been a good leader because he would never have listened to what people *actually* needed instead of what he *thought* they needed. He thought he was different from everyone, but he was still the only one who could see how they needed to live their lives. I get that."

"Then let them live their damned lives!" Dhruv yelled finally. "If you know you can't decide for them, let them decide for themselves! This isn't life or death. It isn't some fucking apocalypse."

"Dhruv." Dan's voice was shaking, and Gracie could feel his tension rising. Dan didn't like confrontation. He didn't want to be here.

She had zero sympathy.

"If you weren't willing to have this out," she told him

sharply, "you shouldn't have come. You don't really want to talk about moving forward, you just want—"

The Aosi staggered forward and sprawled onto the ground. Behind him, a wolf bared its teeth and then threw back its head to howl. It was huge, its fur mottled blood-red and rippling in the wind. A hovering sigil over its head identified it as a rare spawn.

"*Shit.*" Gracie charged into action. "Dan, *up*! Move!"

Dan sprinted away, and the wolf pursued. Dhruv sprang into motion and landed one punch on it, but he was Level 2, so the damage was laughably low.

Gracie slammed sideways into the wolf, relishing the jolt through her haptics, and drew her sword in one smooth motion. She spun and hacked, her teeth bared in a feral grin.

"Listen up, you fucking psychopath, you lost! This is over!"

"Uh, Callista—" Dan started.

"I will *not*—" Gracie gritted out, landing a shield bash "—spend the rest of my fucking *life*—" she landed a less satisfying slash "—looking over my shoulder for you to show up in a dungeon run—" a much more satisfying slash this time "—a random-ass wolf mob—" another shield bash "—OR MY FUCKING APARTMENT!"

The wolf never really stood a chance. She was at a level to be able to take it down, and she was angry as hell. Her health bar was down to one-third and she was panting, but she was still alive when it sprawled at her feet, dead.

Gracie leaned down. "Can you still hear me, motherfucker?"

"Uh. Er." Dan cleared his throat. "Callista—er, Grace."

"Gracie," Gracie said absently.

"Mmm. That's not Harry."

Gracie froze. Her head came up, and she looked at the two of them. "What?" she asked finally.

"That's just...one of the rare wandering spawns," Dan told her.

"Oh," Gracie said faintly.

There was a pause, then Dhruv gave a muffled snort of laughter. Gracie felt a bit of annoyance mixed with her hurt pride, but the amusement hit her in the same moment—and it was far stronger. She choked on a laugh of her own, coughed, and pounded her chest.

"Well, then," she said, after a moment. She knelt to loot the corpse and came up with a single bloody tooth.

"ACHIEVEMENT UNLOCKED," announced the pleasant female voice. "WOLF-SLAYER. Ranking points have been added."

And then all of them were laughing, and they couldn't stop. It was just too much, Gracie thought, a bit helplessly. She hadn't even wanted to be here, and every random chance seemed to be pushing her forward. She seized the chances as they came, of course, but it seemed like she couldn't turn around without tripping over some ranking boost or other.

When they finally stopped laughing, Gracie sighed and looked at the sky. The sun was already dropping again.

"Is that why you brought up the fact that we found you here, not at your house?" Dhruv asked. "Did he actually show up at your place?"

"Yeah." Gracie gazed at them.

"That, we truly never intended." Dan's voice was grave.

"I know." Gracie hadn't even considered that possibility.

"I feel like we should have guessed," Dan said to Dhruv.

"Don't try to anticipate crazy people," Gracie advised. "It'll make you just as crazy." She shrugged. "Look, I don't hate you, and I don't want this to be a fight. But I'm not willing to just forget the past because you want to move forward now. So, how about this: *you* think about what *you* want, then come tell me. Until then, I'm going to hold onto this quest."

She didn't know how to give it up anyway, but *they* didn't have to know that.

They watched her quietly.

"I am not," Gracie told them starkly, "going to let *anyone* destroy this game."

She logged out without waiting for their response.

CHAPTER FOUR

Sam pulled into the parking lot of Dragon Soul Productions and turned off the car. He couldn't quite bring himself to get out, though. He drummed his fingers on the steering wheel and noticed that he was shaking with adrenaline. He'd never been good in situations like this, and boy, was he in one now.

No, that wasn't quite right. This hadn't happened *to* him. He'd done it to himself. The night before, he had orchestrated a pizza party for the express purpose of distracting Dan and Dhruv. It had worked beautifully.

He hadn't been sure of that at first, of course. When the two of them took off like bats out of hell, Sam had been frozen in place, unsure if he should run after them. That would have been an undeniable sign of what was happening, and he still wasn't sure if they'd figured it out.

He hadn't been sure he'd succeeded until he got a text from Jay a few minutes later.

They took the servers down, but we finished first.

Sam had tried to maintain a facade of normalcy and

wound up feeling incredibly ridiculous, wandering around the party with a slice of pizza in one hand and a cup of soda in the other. Waiting to be fired. He'd waited, and he'd waited, and he'd waited some more.

When his shift was over, he had left, half-expecting someone to come running after him.

What did you *do* when you'd committed a firing offense, and no one had noticed yet?

They'd certainly noticed by now. He opened his car door and sighed. He'd done everything he could, and it was time to face the music. His wife wouldn't be pleased, but she would understand. She knew that Sam didn't do things like this without good reason.

And he would be able to find another job.

Still, he was surprised when swiping his badge let him into the building. He stared at the computer for a good five seconds before walking through the turnstile, and when he got to his office, he looked around for booby traps before sitting down.

He glanced at the door. No one was coming down the hallway.

Hmm.

He turned on his computer and opened his email. There was nothing unusual there.

A meeting invite came in with a *bloop*, and Sam jumped and nearly spilled his coffee down his front. He carefully put the mug on the desk before looking at the meeting invite, but he'd seen the location. His heart was already pounding.

Dan's office.

He steeled himself to look once more, confirmed that

the meeting was for right now, and decided to bring his coffee and breakfast sandwich.

If he was getting fired anyway, why not? He took a big bite of his bagel as he walked and washed it down with some coffee. He was really going to miss everyone here, but he was trying not to think about that.

And then he walked into Dan's office—to see Jay.

"Thay?" he managed through a mouthful of bagel.

Jay had been engaged in a stare-off with Dhruv, but he looked around at this. "Sam."

Sam swallowed hastily. "Hi." He set his food down on the table and reached out to shake Jay's hand, then changed his mind and hugged him. "How have you been?"

"Good." Jay gave a wary look at the other two. "So, uh..."

"Yes," Dan said. "Please, sit." He shot a look at Dhruv, which Sam identified as the same one he gave his four-year-old when she had a crayon in one hand and a nice, blank expanse of wall in front of her. "Don't you dare."

Sam glanced at Dan, who looked equably back. Dan was well over thirty and eternally sleep-deprived, but he somehow managed to look fresh-faced, like a rumpled college student who had never quite learned how to use a comb.

Dan looked at Jay. "Last night, Sam asked to speak to me about you. About bringing you back on board."

Sam froze. *Oh, no.* He had in fact done that, but he had done so as part of the distraction. When Jay shot a look at him, he took a big bite of his bagel instead of looking back.

"He made several compelling points," Dan continued, seeing that Sam did not seem inclined to pick up the thread of conversation. "Your record was incredibly good, and you consistently received high review scores as a manager. In similar situations, there is usually a pattern of problems, but there was not one here."

He paused, perhaps waiting for a response from Jay.

Jay looked at Sam, however. "You…didn't mention this to me."

"I didn't want to promise anything," Sam mumbled. It held together as an excuse.

Dan nodded approvingly. "I'm glad you came to us first. It was a trying night."

Now they had come to it. Sam sat up warily.

"As you are almost certainly aware," Dan said to Sam, "and as *you* are, of course, fully aware," a pointed look at Jay, "Callista finished Harry's embedded quest last night."

"Mmm," Sam managed. "Yes, I saw there was a server outage?"

Dan's expression flickered slightly. "Yes," he said, but did not elaborate. He gazed at Jay for a long moment. "Now, as you know, we did not want…Gracie…to finish the quest. Part of that was due to the havoc it wreaked on the ranking system, but part of it was also that we have no way to know the scope of what has just happened."

"There is one person who knows," Jay pointed out. He sat back in his chair, and his eyes flicked between Dan and Dhruv. "Have you asked him?"

"I think you know we haven't," Dhruv replied.

"Surely you can understand," Dan chimed in, cutting back in before things could escalate. For a moment, he looked deeply weary.

"I'm not sure anymore," Jay said. "Harry keeps being

treated as this total wild card, but as far as I know, neither of you has gone out of your way to actually *talk* to the man."

"Gracie has," Dan said silkily. "Well, *he* spoke to *her*."

"You knew about that?" Jay demanded.

"We found out about it last night," Dan said. He folded his hands in his lap. "When we spoke to her."

"When you *what*?" Jay asked far too nicely.

"Believe it or not, everyone came out of it with their bones unbroken and their egos unshattered," Dan snapped, finally losing his patience. "The point is, we have begun an open dialog with her, and we brought you here to offer you your job back. I will not insult you by lying—we did hope not to be in this situation. However, since we *are* here, it is necessary for us to change."

"A particularly heartfelt apology would be a good start," Jay said.

Sam shot him a look that said, "Goddamn, man."

Jay sighed. "I'm sorry. That was uncalled for."

"Accurate, though," Dhruv weighed in. He crossed his arms and stared at Jay. "I argued in your favor as well. You say what you mean. I like that."

"The only thing we have to consider," Dan said, "is whether or not you feel…comfortable…returning. Well, two: how we deal with any similar issues in the future."

"Just so we're clear," Jay said, "you're admitting I was right?"

"No," Dan said flatly. "We made considered decisions to contain an unknown threat. We did not owe it to you to follow some democratic ideal of what to do. We are a business, Jay. Our obligation is to our funders."

Jay said nothing to this, but Sam could see him fighting not to snap at Dan.

"So, perhaps the question is," Dan continued, "are you willing to work for a company that is funded this way? You're knowledgeable, Jay. You're a good boss, and your employees have missed you. Your own boss came to speak to us, asking us to reconsider. That's not a small thing." He paused. "And you did what you did, in part because of your care for the game," he admitted grudgingly.

Jay considered this. "Yes," he said finally. "I would like to come back."

Sam said a silent prayer of thanks. He hadn't considered it possible that Dan and Dhruv would seriously consider his suggestion or that Jay would, but he was glad it was working out.

"Excellent," Dan said. "I want to set the clear expectation that in the future, you will come to us with any similar concerns and that we will take them under advisement. We may or may not make the decision you are hoping for. Is that workable?"

Jay did not hesitate. "Yes."

"Good." Dan smiled. "I will let HR know you've been reinstated. Would you be willing to start tomorrow?"

Now Jay did take a moment to consider. "Yes," he said finally.

Dan nodded. "Thank you both for your time." It was a clear dismissal.

Outside the room, Sam and Jay walked in silence. By mutual agreement, they made their way to the parking lot and over to Jay's semi-battered old two-door. Jay waited by the car and gave Sam a curious look, and Sam sighed.

"I was trying to distract them last night. I didn't think he'd take the suggestion *seriously*."

Jay burst out laughing. "So all of this—you thought it was—"

"I left my bagel," Sam said, staring back at the building. "Son of a bitch!"

Jay snorted and wiped his eyes. "So, you threw a Hail Mary into the stands and someone caught it."

"Pretty much," Sam agreed after taking a moment to consider it. "And you actually *want* to come back?"

"More or less." Jay shrugged.

"Jay, *don't* do anything stupid."

"I won't," Jay assured him with the most insincere smile Sam had ever seen.

Sam sighed. "I'll see you tomorrow, then. Go get some rest."

"The hell I will," Jay said bluntly. "I'm going to go find out exactly what they said to Gracie last night."

CHAPTER FIVE

Thad had been a terrible boss. Now that Jamie was gone, he could admit that. Moody and competitive, Thad *needed* to be the best in the room, and he couldn't cope with anyone else even coming close.

It was probably why the Demon Syndicate wouldn't stay a top-tier guild, Jamie reflected. As soon as Thad found the best players, he would either drive them away with his competitiveness or keep them from becoming the best they could be.

There *was* one thing to be said for Thad's sulkiness, however. Jamie had been able to pack up his room and get out of the building without having to talk to him. The others had hovered nearby, no one quite willing to take the risk of helping Jamie pack, but they had all given him handshakes or hugs on the way out. Some of the newbies looked particularly terrified. It was difficult when a guild lost their top healer.

Jamie rode the high of his decision until the cab driver asked him where he wanted to go.

Then he realized he had no idea, *and* he was carrying all of his worldly possessions in two suitcases. He stared blankly, but the cab driver, who had apparently seen similar situations before, drove Jamie to a nearby coffee shop near the bus line, offering comforting platitudes about how women weren't worth the trouble and telling Jamie he could live a better life as a bachelor. Apparently, he'd decided that Jamie had been thrown out of his apartment after a fight with a girlfriend.

Jamie was too shell-shocked to correct him.

In the coffee shop, the solution came to him in the form of a text message.

Just checking in, it read. **I know you're probably getting reamed out right now. Just let us know how it shakes out—and if you need help**.

Jamie stared at the message for a long time, trying to decide if it was a genuine offer. In the end, he threw caution to the winds and typed back: **Actually…**

Which was how he found himself walking out of Sea-Tac Airport a scant six hours later, shivering in the drizzly cold and peering into the passing cars until a man flagged him down with a smile.

"Hey," Kevin said, stepping out of a Tesla Model 3.

Jamie gaped. He was unusually attractive, a fact that had always made him more self-conscious than proud. It had been especially awkward when Brightstar wanted to use Jamie for all of their promo photos and Thad had glowered in the background.

He didn't hold a candle to Kevin, though. He was 5'8" or so and had dark blond hair. Kevin's jawline might have been chiseled from stone, and his clothes, perfectly tailored, fell over a body that spoke of a personal trainer and a carefully-curated diet.

Kevin raised one perfect eyebrow at Jamie's dumbstruck expression.

"I, uh…" Jamie cleared his throat and recovered. "Was kind of expecting a Piskie with pink hair."

Kevin burst out laughing and came over to clasp Jamie's hand before loading his bags into the trunk of the car. He opened the passenger door for Jamie before heading back around to slide into the driver's seat.

"You hungry?" he asked.

"A little." Jamie's stomach grumbled loudly. "Ravenous, actually. I just can't face being in a restaurant."

"Takeout, it is." Kevin handed his phone over and pulled away from the curb. "If you go into my favorites there, you'll see the places that deliver. Whatever looks good to you. I'm easy."

"You're getting a call." Jamie handed the phone back.

Kevin looked at the screen and grimaced. "Hit Ignore, would you?" When he saw Jamie's curious expression, he gave a half-embarrassed shrug. "Long story."

"I have literally nothing else to do," Jamie pointed out.

"You have food to order," Kevin reminded him.

Jamie ordered them both food and then craned around to look at the gray clouds and the Seattle skyline. His own phone rang, and he looked down to see Evan's number. He hadn't ever given Brightstar an official resignation, he realized now.

Whoops.

Kevin's phone rang again the next moment, showing the same number as before, and both men started laughing.

They were wearing the same expression of resignation and guiltiness.

"I'll tell you if you tell me," Jamie offered. "Of course, you know what's going on with me."

"You didn't exactly explain it," Kevin pointed out. "But I gather you hightailed it out of there after the boss went down. It's good that you managed to get your stuff. Assuming that *is* your stuff." He looked over. "You didn't steal a bunch of VR equipment, did you?"

"No." Jamie laughed, then shivered. "Uh, can I turn the heat up?"

"Sure. Let's stop somewhere to get you a sweatshirt, too. I'd offer you one of mine, but you're *tall*." Kevin looked around, clearly thinking, then pulled into the exit lane to head to a nearby mall.

"And what about you...?" Jamie asked pointedly.

"This feels like an uneven trade." Kevin sighed as he took the exit in a quick, controlled curve. "Eh, it's no big deal. I just met, you know...the One."

"What?" Jamie looked down at the phone. "Do you... shouldn't you call him back?"

"No, because he's boring as sin," Kevin said bluntly.

"I thought you said—"

"He *is*," Kevin said. "He's exactly what I've been looking for for years. Thought he didn't exist. Loves the same shows I do, doesn't mind the video games, has a good career, likes to travel, great taste, all of it. And I found him —and he bores me to fucking tears." He sighed as he pulled into the parking lot of the mall. "I just got a promotion at work, and I have the job I've wanted, also for years, and I hate *that*, too." He shut off the car and considered for a moment. "You don't need to hear all of this right now. You've had a *day*. Let's get you some warmer clothes and head home for food." He got out of the car.

"Or..." Jamie said, also getting out, "we could get me warmer clothes, get a bottle of tequila, and *then* go home for food." He gave a grin. "Our lives both went to shit."

"So let's get shitfaced?" Kevin asked, looking bemused.

"Pretty much. Get all the ranting out of our systems."

"You're on." Kevin led the way into the mall. "But I'm going to teach you to like port because tequila is disgusting."

"That's because you've never had good tequila," Jamie asserted confidently. "Trust me, I'll have you converted by tomorrow."

"A lot of people have said that to me over the years," Kevin told him philosophically. "Of course, they were all female. And talking about something else."

Jamie guffawed but sobered quickly. "Thanks for giving me a place to crash."

"Anytime," Kevin said easily.

The best thing about having Dan and Dhruv as enemies, Harry had decided, was that they were clever enough to make good connections. They understood the playing field well, and their instincts were well-honed.

He could use their hunches now to lay his groundwork. They had identified the relevant players, and it was up to Harry now to make better use of those players than they could.

After all, he understood now that their defiance was only to be expected. He could not ask for anything more than that. It was the nature of humans to resist kings, so a king must be ready to hold his throne.

Callista has your throne. The thought was unwelcome and made him clench his teeth in frustration.

That was temporary. There was enough chaos in the world to push *anyone* to the throne, but most of them could not hold it. What would set Harry apart was the fact that he could. No matter how many people tried to stand in his way, he would find his rightful place. This was a test, nothing more.

He did not even entertain the thought that the test would find him unworthy. These tests were nothing more than smelting metal to burn away the impurities, and when they were passed, only the king would remain, stronger than before.

His choice—his first choice—was simple. There was someone else who had been wronged as he had, and who knew Callista.

What should have been easy, however, fell to ruin almost at once.

"Hello?" The man's voice was cautious. "Who is this?"

"Jay?" Harry kept his voice casual, although his pulse sped up. He was so close. Things were falling into place perfectly.

How had he ever doubted himself?

"Who is this?" Jay repeated.

"Harry," Harry said. "I take it you know that name."

"I know you showed up at Gracie's apartment," Jay replied, and his voice was cold as ice. "I know you made more than a few people's lives a living hell. What I *don't* know is why. Why you're doing any of this."

"I'm happy to explain," Harry said. "After all, that's why I called."

"That's..." Jay's voice trailed off. "Bullshit," he said finally. "If you wanted to explain, you'd be calling Gracie. You'd be calling Dan and Dhruv. I'm not someone you need to explain to...unless you want something from me."

Harry decided to welcome this. "I *need* something," he corrected. "Not want, need. Something you need as well."

Jay said absolutely nothing. There was the distant sound of a car stopping and the brief dinging of a key in a lock. Jay was still there—Harry could hear him—but he wasn't saying anything.

Harry took a deep breath and prayed for patience. "You understood that Dan and Dhruv weren't good leaders. You spoke the truth, hoping that they would understand it and correct their course, and instead, they fired you. They never even apologized, did they?"

Still Jay said nothing.

Harry was beginning to lose his temper. "You follow Callista because she offers you an alternative."

Jay snorted now. It was clear he didn't think much of that assessment. "How about, instead of telling me what you think you know about me, you tell me what you want?"

"You know that Dan and Dhruv—"

"No," Jay said flatly. "No persuasion, no backstory. Tell me what you want in plain language, or I will hang up this phone." There was a pause, then he added with a half-laugh, "I wondered why no one had just talked to you, and I get it now. You're insufferable."

Harry gritted his teeth and tried to say the words Jay wanted to hear. "I *must* persuade you, do you understand that? Or *Metamorphosis Online* will be destroyed. I know you don't want that. I know Callista doesn't want that. I suppose Dan and Dhruv do not, either, but all they see is a cash cow. Tell me what you want, Jay, and I will—"

"Insufferable," Jay repeated. He was clearly smiling. Harry could picture him shaking his head. "You are fundamentally incapable of seeing other people as anything other than objects. Obstacle courses. You can't figure out how to work *with* someone." He paused. "All you can see is what you want, so you dress it up in morals and make it some epic struggle. You're as bad as they are."

The line went dead.

Harry stared down at the phone, his lip curling in anger.

Jay wasn't going to help him. Jay had been corrupted, turned to a useless, *pointless* cause: loyalty to a false queen. A true king would be resisted, Harry knew that, but didn't he also deserve loyalty? Didn't he deserve someone standing at his side? If Callista was a false queen—which she was—then why did *she* have a team at her back?

There was a moment of doubt, but only one.

Then Harry's head came up. Kingship, true kingship, was lonely. He had known it when he wrote Yesuan's quest, and he was beginning to understand the truth of it now.

But where Yesuan had failed, he would succeed.

He just needed a new ally.

CHAPTER SIX

Gracie woke up to an empty apartment and sunlight streaming in the windows. She'd slept until almost noon, which was hardly a surprise, given that she'd been up so late. When she went to bed after speaking to Dan and Dhruv, it was to stare up at the darkness. Sleep stubbornly eluded her, and she wasn't sure when she'd finally dropped off.

Alex, of course, would be at work, mainlining coffee. She smiled as she stumbled out into the living room, finger-combing her hair into some semblance of order. It wouldn't have felt right to do last night's quest without Alex there.

The coffee that had been fresh that morning was long-since cold, but there was a waxed-paper bag on the counter. Gracie peeked inside and gave a grin. A bakery had opened nearby, and Alex had mentioned wanting to try their pastries. Apparently, he'd decided to do so this morning. A note next to the bag said,

I recommend the bear claw. I seriously considered eating yours and just not telling you I'd gotten you one.

Gracie chortled as she pulled the bear claw out and took a bite, then her eyes drifted closed. From the crunch of the almonds to the warmth of the cinnamon sugar, it was heavenly. She put some coffee in the microwave and slouched back to the bedroom to retrieve her phone.

All of last night was coming back to her in a rush now, and she found herself blushing. None of it felt real. Yesterday, she'd been considering avoiding the Yesuan's Haunt run entirely and pining secretly over Jay.

Today…

She thought back to the times in Night's Edge, to the boss fights they'd gotten through side-by-side in the melee. She'd saved his ass a dozen times, and he'd done the same for her. When there was a bear charging at you, or a giant with a huge mace, it didn't matter that it was all pixels. It took courage to stare the boss down, and courage to sacrifice yourself for someone else.

She'd done the same for everyone in the guild at one time or another, but she knew it was different with Jay.

She just hadn't dreamed he felt the same.

She came back to herself staring at the wall, the bear claw forgotten in one hand and the mug of coffee forgotten in the other. Her cheeks were on fire, and when her phone buzzed, she practically leapt out of her skin. Setting the coffee and pastry on the counter, she fished her phone out of her pocket and flushed an even brighter red at the name on the screen.

You up yet, lazy?

Rude, she typed back. She took a picture of herself with the bear claw, agonized over her disheveled appearance, and deleted it.

She really sucked at this.

For your information, she told him, **I have been up for at LEAST 10 minutes, and I'm having a very healthy breakfast.** She sent a picture of the coffee and bear claw.

Like a boss, Jay texted back. Dots appeared to show that he was typing. They were there for a long while, but all that appeared was: **Do you have time to talk?**

Gracie's stomach seemed to fall out of her chest, and she swallowed hard as she stared at the phone.

Another message appeared: **Dan and Dhruv said they talked to you. There's some stuff you should know about that whole thing.**

A pause, then, **Anyway, if you have time, I want you to have at least one day off from this shit if you want it.**

Gracie sighed with relief, shook her head, and gave herself a stern talking to. Jay had been *happy* to hear what she said last night since he felt the same way. She needed to get over this stupid idea that everything was going to fall apart.

Nah, she texted back. **If evil doesn't sleep, neither do we.**

Hahahaha

Meet you online? she asked him.

I'm not sure that's wise

I'm a queen now, remember? And I want to find out what my powers are. Besides, she added, **even if they CAN hear us, I want them to know we're comparing notes.**

It's not QUITE that simple, Jay texted back, **but I'll see**

you there. Where are you?

Outside Kithara, Gracie told him. **I'll see you there.**

She wolfed down the rest of her bear claw, taking gulps of coffee between bites, and pulled her hair back before logging into the game. She'd left her VR suit crumpled on the ground last night, walking away from Dan and Dhruv and *Metamorphosis* and all of it. Now, she hesitated before putting it on. Jay was right; a day off would have been nice.

But she was right, too—she wasn't going to take a day off and come back to find that her enemies had closed ranks and she was barred from the one place she felt truly at home.

The sun was sliding down toward the horizon when she logged in, and she stood in the tall grass and waited. It wasn't long before Jay appeared on her mini-map, and she turned to watch him approach, feeling the instinctive leap of recognition at the sight of him.

He stopped for a moment, looking at her, then emoted a smile before he walked the rest of the way.

"What?" Gracie said, smiling back.

"Nothing."

"It's not nothing." She was grinning.

Jay took a breath deep enough that she saw the movement in his avatar. "I wish I could kiss you," he said finally. Almost sheepishly, he added, "Being in armor makes me braver."

Gracie gave a peal of laughter. "So, what, we have to have all our dates at a Renaissance Faire or something?"

Jay started laughing as well. "See, that's what I like about you—you're a problem solver."

Gracie reached out to give him an affectionate shove

and nearly overbalanced. "Crap, I keep forgetting you aren't actually *there*. We'll, uh..." She swallowed hard. What was she nervous about? "We'll have to fix that at some point." She could hear her blood pounding in her ears.

"I'd like that," Jay said, and the sound of his voice sent shivers up and down her spine. "You know, it was very hard to stay focused in the meeting this morning."

"Mmm?" Gracie glanced at him, then processed what he'd said. "The meeting... Wait, did you speak to Dan and Dhruv *today*? Like, in person?"

"Yes, I did." Jay rubbed at the back of his neck. "Uh, okay, so...I did something. I can undo it; don't worry."

"What did you do?" Gracie raised an eyebrow before remembering that the expression wouldn't come through. "Look, I can't imagine you doing something really crazy without checking in with the rest of us. Right? Jay, tell me I'm right."

"You're right." He was smiling. "I...I guess Sam talked to them about giving me my job back, so they called me in to make an offer. I took them up on it."

"*What?*" Gracie's jaw dropped. "Wait, back up—"

"It's a long story. I'll tell you more later, but basically, Sam pointed out that I was a popular employee and did good work, and they said they were willing to give me a second chance."

"A 'second chance'?" Gracie repeated. Her tone was dangerous.

"Oh, I know." Jay nodded. "Infuriating, right? *They're* giving *me* a second chance when I was the one who was right all along? Yeah. But I thought..." He sighed.

"I don't think they can hear us," Gracie said. "Harry

would have made sure he was protected."

"Hmm." Jay considered. "They said they were offering an olive branch," he said finally. "That was what they told me, at least. They hadn't wanted you to win like you did, but you had, and they were going to find a new way forward. I thought that was worth entertaining. I want them to keep trying to work with people they don't agree with instead of trying to undercut them."

"That makes sense." Gracie set off through the grass, jerking her head for him to follow. The sun was setting, and she knew all of a sudden where she wanted to go. "And the part you're not sure about saying out loud?"

Jay laughed. "There were times when it would have helped us to have someone on the inside. Do you remember telling me that? When you said it, I'd just quit, and I felt like an idiot. You were right."

"Hmm." Gracie considered that. The hill was winding upwards, and above them, the sky was beginning to fade.

"You're going back to the starting zone," Jay said, realizing where they were. "To where we first met."

"We first met over there," Gracie said distractedly, pointing.

"Oh. Ah…" He cleared his throat. "Funny story about that."

Gracie stopped and looked at him. "Funny story?"

"You remember talking to the hill warden?" Jay asked. When she stared at him silently, he actually took a step back. "Oh, dear. I thought I'd told you."

"You were the *hill warden?*" Gracie demanded. "No, you did *not* tell me. *You* told me the riddle? You started the whole damned thing?"

"I was just inside the character," Jay clarified. "It was programmed to say that to anyone who asked about the kobolds or what was in that direction. I know I told it to at least a couple of other people, too. No one else bothered to try to figure it out, though."

Gracie sighed and then started laughing. "Just when I think this whole thing couldn't get any more ridiculous. Wait, the hill warden is there now."

"Mmhmm. There might or might not be an actual person in there."

"That's creepy as shit, man. It's like walking through a store filled with mannequins and thinking some of them might be looking at you." Gracie started walking again, giving the hill warden a wide berth. "Okay, so *you* were the hill warden. Huh."

"To be clear, I was pretty specifically *not* supposed to create a character and go around adventuring with people," Jay said. "But I hadn't seen anyone else go fight in that temple. None of us even had. We were all trying to get to Kithara and get new gear and stuff—see all the high-level content, you know? So I followed you."

"Creeper," Gracie chided affectionately.

"Yeah, see, you say that, but guys are terrified of being creeps."

She looked at him. "Sorry. So you work for Dragon Soul again?"

"Yeah." Jay caught up with her. He looked at the sky, where stars were beginning to appear. "I know they won't exactly *trust* me, but I'll at least be there. I'll have an idea of what's going on. We'll have a link."

"I like that," Gracie assured him. She headed down the

other slope, making her way toward the temple. In the moonlight, it looked almost exactly as it had that first night. She felt a jarring sense of déjà vu.

They didn't speak as they approached the temple. The outside had been cleaned, which only made the chips in the stone more noteworthy, but it had also been hung with paper flags and little ornaments made from rocks and twigs. After a moment of hesitation, Gracie pushed open the door and stepped inside.

The temple was nearly deserted, but fires burned in low braziers, the stone was all clean once more, and there was the sound of distant music and running water. Gracie looked around, nodding to the kobold monks moving around the room, then walked down the sloping path into the belly of the temple.

"You know, I came in here." Jay's voice was low, but it still made her jump, "and I saw that room, but there was no door for me. No passageway either."

Gracie flashed him a smile. "You're not the queen."

Jay laughed.

They came into the lower chamber to find it awash with blue light. The stone was radiant, filling the air with a glow that was somehow soft and thick with magic. Gracie reached out to swish her fingers through it, half-expecting it to feel like water, and shook her head at her own foolishness.

"So this is where it started," Jay said. He looked around.

"While they fought to the death upstairs," Gracie said, "finishing a fight I'd started." To her surprise, her throat was tight. "You can't right wrongs without losing something in the struggle. It's not fair."

Jay said nothing, just looked at her.

"They were taking back what was theirs," she explained. Then she realized what was tugging at her mind. "Like Harry tried to take back what was his."

"It isn't his anymore," Jay said. "It doesn't belong to any of them. It belongs to you now."

"No." Gracie shook her head. "It doesn't belong to me, Jay. I'm not a queen, I'm a steward. I'm going to keep it safe."

"From Dan and Dhruv?" Jay asked.

"Maybe." She frowned. "I don't know, actually. I just know…something's coming. And we have to be ready."

Jay nodded at her.

"Hey, guys!" The voice that came over the guild channel was upbeat and made both of them jump and swear.

"Uh…hey, Cas." Gracie pressed a hand over her heart. Then her brain caught up with her. "Whoa. You're…not fired?"

"Oh, no, I'm—well, I don't know what I am. I'm not *there* anymore." Caspian sounded excessively happy, and—now that Gracie was listening, more than a little drunk. "Kevin's letting me crash with him."

"What up?" Kevin was also slurring his words. "Turns out tequila's pretty good."

Gracie laughed despite herself. "Oh, dear. Anyone have any quests they want to do?"

There was a drunken chorus of yesses.

"Okay, then Jay and I will help—*if*, and I mean this seriously, you both go get a big glass of water first." She shook her head. "Otherwise, tomorrow's going to be rough. Go. Drink up. Chop-chop."

CHAPTER SEVEN

It was a solid five minutes before Caspian and Kevin got back, and when they did, there was a lot of swearing and a few muffled thuds.

"Guys?" Gracie asked. "Everyone okay over there?" She and Jay were close to Kithara now, making their way along the winding road. The sky was still dark, and the stars were brilliant.

"Yes," Kevin said much too quickly. "It's fine. Everything's fine; we're all fine here. How are you?"

"He fell over," Caspian said in a stage whisper.

"I go pick your ridiculously tall ass up from the airport, and this is the thanks I get?" Kevin sounded aggrieved, which was hilarious in the Piskie voice filter. "He got me drunk on tequila," he added mournfully. "I don't even *like* tequila."

"You drank an awful lot of it for someone who doesn't like it," Caspian said smugly. To the others, he added, "The only people who don't like tequila are the ones who haven't had the good stuff."

"Sure," Gracie agreed doubtfully, her mouth twitching. "So, where do you two slap-happy kids want to go adventuring?"

"*I* don't know," Caspian said. "I just wanted to—" His voice cut off very suddenly.

"Cas?" Jay asked.

"Sec."

A moment later, Gracie's phone buzzed. She popped her headset off, frowned at it, and opened a private channel to Jay. "Caspian says Kevin's having a hard time and he wanted to come online and cheer him up rather than having him be all morose and drunk."

"Oh?"

"Well, what he actually said was *'Kev id drubk sad we should cheer hio op,'* so I paraphrased. I'm pretty sure I got it right, though."

Jay was laughing on the other end, his character's shoulders shaking. "Yeah, I'd say that's a solid interpretation." He switched back to the main channel. "Kev. Didn't you have some quests to do?"

"I don't think so." Kevin's voice was still slurred. "Lemme check. Moment. Why the fuck can't I open my quests? Goddammit."

Gracie grinned. They had gotten to the huge gates that led into Kithara, and she could see Caspian and Fys standing in the very middle of the road. Since it was midday in real time, the servers weren't very full, but a few people were looking at the tabards the two were wearing.

Everything associated with Gracie was becoming noteworthy.

"*That's* interesting," Kevin said after a moment.

"What's interesting?" Gracie got closer and waved.

"Did you check your messages?" Kevin asked. "Because I just did, and I *just* caught a glimpse of one about a new king...which disappeared a moment later."

"Of course, he did that," Gracie said, rolling her eyes. "Of *course* he set the server up to send everyone a message about how he was here to rule over them like a benevolent dictator. I bet he expected everyone to go into paroxysms of joy."

"'Aa sounds dirry," Caspian slurred.

Gracie gave a somewhat exasperated huff of laughter. "All right, no more tequila for you two."

"No," Caspian agreed. "'S all gone."

"You drank a whole *bottle*?" Jay said, sounding horrified. "Good God, how are you two upright?"

"He's really *big*," Kevin explained. His avatar gestured widely, opening her arms like an alligator's jaws. "Just... really *tall*. Lot of person there. Doesn't get drunk easy."

Caspian said nothing but he was swaying drunkenly.

"Right," Gracie said. "Well, I'm excited to see what's different about my character, because it looks like I have some new menus available. Also, *someone* should keep an eye on you two, so you don't...I don't know, rob a bank or whatever."

"Is that what straight people do when they get drunk?" Kevin asked suspiciously. "What is even going on with the heteros?"

"I've never robbed a bank," Caspian said.

"Mmm." It sounded like Kevin had more to say on the matter, but he didn't share it, whatever it was.

Gracie tabbed through her menus as the rest of them came up with a location, so she set her character to follow Fys—the Piskie was so short that it felt like she was walking around on her own—and examined the tools she now had available.

She couldn't believe she hadn't looked last night. The setup was completely different now. There were actions to ban players, unban them, mute them, and hide them from one another. She could award ranking points or take them away. She could dissolve guilds. There were also controls that looked as though they dealt with the internal metrics of the game's various playing and non-playing races.

"This is crazy," Gracie said quietly.

"Come on through the portal," Jay told her. "Then you can show us the crazy."

"Right." Gracie nodded and stepped through the portal. She barely took notice of where she was going and laughed when she saw that it was Night's Edge. "Of course, you chose this."

"Of course, we did," Jay said, sounding pleased. "I still think there's more here than we found the last time."

"Hmm." Gracie looked around, then put away the menus. "One second, I want to try something. Wait here."

She trotted off down the sloping streets until she found one particular alley. Here they had once found…

Ah, yes. A rustling sound came from the dark. Gracie tilted her head to the side and unsheathed her sword and shield. "Hello. Let's try this again, shall we?"

The spider came at her in a rush, easily twice as tall as

she was, mandibles clicking and eyes glowing red. Gracie gave a yell she hoped would pass as being warlike instead of frightened and bashed her shield into its round body before thrusting the sword straight in. There was a scream and a *lot* of glowing blue blood, and the spider's body disappeared.

Gracie turned, trying not to hunch her shoulders. She wasn't *actually* covered in blue spider blood, after all. Not really. Nope.

Ew.

"So, I one-shot things now," she reported as she sheathed her sword. "But apparently, I do *not* have a magic clean-up button."

"Let me tell you," Jay said queasily, "those liquid dynamics animations are *really* realistic."

"I'll be right back," Caspian managed. There was a thud as his VR headset dropped to the ground.

"Huh," Kevin mused. "I guess the kid gets drunk after all. What d'you know? I'll be right back. I'm going to bring him more water, and maybe some saltines."

"Solid," Jay said. He wandered over to one of the lanterns on the walls and glanced at Gracie. "Hope you don't think I'm a coward, but there is no way I'm hanging out in that alley."

Gracie laughed and came to join him.

"So," Jay said. "Tell me about the new controls."

"They're insane," Gracie replied. "You can ban people, mute them—specifically mute connections between them. It's like a dictator's wet dream, honestly."

Jay must have taken the opportunity to take a sip of water because there was a snort, then the sound of someone trying desperately to clear his throat. "Okay, file *that* with sentences I never thought I'd hear."

"It was the easiest way to describe it."

"Easy, hell." He crossed his arms. "You have an uncanny sense for when I've decided to try to drink something, and you do your utmost to have me get it up my nose."

Gracie looked away airily. "I have no idea what you mean."

"Ooooof *course*, you don't." Jay had his character lean against the wall. "So, you're basically a god and now you can wrath-of-god anyone who disagrees with you."

"That's Harry in a nutshell," Gracie said grumpily.

"There's...something else you should know." Jay recapped his phone conversation with Harry, speaking quickly. He shook his head when he was done. "I should have tried to get more out of him. Played along."

"Maybe," Gracie said after a pause. "But I think that's a fine line to walk. He's smart, Jay. He might just as easily play you as having you play him. And it's not necessarily bad for him to see people being loyal to one another. I'd rather have him wondering if he's missing something. If there's another way to be." She shook her head. "Honestly, I think it was for the best. Just don't play his game."

Jay emoted a smile at her. "It's a weight off my mind to hear you say that. Honestly, with everything else that's been going on, I forgot about Harry being a jerk."

"I see what you mean," Gracie pointed out. "I often forget to mention that the sun is shining."

Jay guffawed, but when he spoke, he sounded worried. "Gracie, you know he's not going to give up. Him, Dan, and Dhruv... Hell, I don't know, even the other guilds."

"I'll just ban all of them," Gracie said with a shrug. She shuddered. "Ugh, even saying that made me feel greasy. Blech."

"Yeah, you don't have that villain *flair* to you," Kevin said. "Good news, guys, Caspian expelled the demons."

"Hi," Caspian said weakly.

"Are you okay, man?" Gracie asked. "You could go to sleep if you wanted…"

"Nah, I feel much better," Caspian said. "Really. Better out than in, as my grandfather always said."

"He sounds fun," Gracie commented. "Well, if we're looking for something strange. What do you say we head to the water?"

Everyone agreed at once, and they trooped down the hill, Kevin singing a sea shanty that started on the topic of Barrett's privateers and segued mid-song into *The Wreck of the Edmund Fitzgerald*.

He had a surprisingly good voice.

When they reached the water, Gracie hesitated only a moment before wading into it. The sounds of sloshing greeted her, and she almost imagined she could feel the cold water swirling around her.

When she plunged underwater at last, she gasped.

Above the waterline, Night's Edge was a study in life after disaster. It was hopeful and heartbreaking all at once.

Below the waterline, it was entirely different. The world lit up. Stately architecture showed a city that was still whole, with merpeople swimming to and fro along the streets. Ahead, in a temple, something shone a deep, steady blue.

"That's disappointing," Jay said. "When I heard you gasp, I hoped there would be something cool down here."

Gracie turned to gape at him. "What are you seeing?"

"Old ruins." He looked around. "Why, what are *you* seeing?"

Gracie didn't answer. She turned around and swam for the blue light, afraid that if she didn't find out what it was now, the illusion would disintegrate and leave her with only the ruins Jay saw.

It was so bright inside the mer temple that she could barely see. She swam closer to the light with her head down and her arm over her face. Luckily, the suit knew where her arm was and gave her a bit of respite, but the light was still streaming forward.

When it disappeared, she flailed and looked around.

She was inside a bubble. She could see it around her, shining out into the water.

In front of her was an altar draped in blue cloth. She walked forward, eyes locked on the object that lay there: an axe, plain and unadorned, very clearly meant for death. *Never forget what a weapon is,* her mind told her.

She reached out to pick it up and smiled when green runes skittered across its surface.

I'm going to find all your secrets, Harry. Every one of them.

CHAPTER EIGHT

"No one else is ready!" Thad's fists clenched in mid-air. He clenched his teeth too, doing everything in his power not to snarl at the Brightstar executives that they didn't have the first idea of what was going on.

"We're not telling you *how* to do it." Richard, the VP of Strategic Marketing, was by nature a patient man, but his voice had the crisp edge that meant he was beginning to lose his temper. "We do not micromanage. We are simply telling you what needs to happen.

"And *I* am telling *you* that it isn't possible. Not this month, not this quickly. We can't get a new top-tier healer onto the team in that timeframe without spending a *lot* more than you want to spend. We'd have to get one from Blood Magic or Shrinra Corp."

"We're not telling you *how* to do it," Richard repeated. The edge in his voice was stronger this time. "We are simply saying that we are not getting the return we expected. We had a clear goal of becoming the leading guild within six months. We thought you had achieved this, but it was clearly not a lasting success. *That* is what we need to see."

"You need to *build*," Thad told him desperately. He wanted to run his fingers through his hair, but Evan was there—because of course he was—and Thad knew he couldn't appear weak. He stared at the speakerphone and fumbled for something to say. Anything that would buy him time. "There's no competitive e-sport where one team dominates consistently. The top-tier teams sometimes have streaks, but it's always a toss-up."

There was a pause while he allowed himself to hope that Richard understood. It wasn't even a lie, but Thad knew there was desperation in his voice. He had a vivid memory of assuring them that he could make the Demon Syndicate a dominant guild in *Metamorphosis Online*, that they would have winning streaks no other guild could replicate. They'd been impressed, and he'd gotten the job as guild leader.

"So you're telling me you can't do it," Richard said finally. He put an ever-so-slight emphasis on the word "you."

"That's not what I'm saying," Thad replied desperately.

"Then what *are* you saying, Mr. Matthews? This meeting is going in circles."

"I'm saying I can build a strong team," Thad replied. An icy cold was spreading through him, which would have been welcome if he weren't sure that it was panic instead of calm. "First of all, any team will have turnover. People will leave, and adaptation needs to happen. Second, we are in an unusual situation, as evidenced by the fact that Dragon Soul cannot control the rankings anymore. What I need is time to adapt to this. To raise another strong healer so that we can be top tier again."

"Mr. Matthews." Richard spoke so quickly after Thad did that it was clear he had not cared a whit for anything Thad said. "When you were hired, you promised to give us a dominant guild in return for our investment. Brightstar does not have a small advertising budget, but running this guild is expensive. We need to see measurable results, or we will need to iterate. To be absolutely clear, the first iteration we will attempt will be a change in leadership. Do you understand?"

Thad swallowed hard. "Yes," he said quietly.

"Excellent. You have until the end of the month, Mr. Matthews. We expect Demon Syndicate to win the next Month First badge. If you do, we will consider continuing your contract. Thank you for being on this meeting, everyone. I will talk to you all later."

The call ended and Thad stared at the speaker incredulously, shame heating his cheeks. He'd been treated like a child. Richard had not allowed him to say another word after the pronouncement of that *ridiculous* goal.

Month First. Without a top healer.

"I know you have several healers on the team," Evan said hesitantly after a moment.

Thad's head whipped around. Evan was always saying things like that. He didn't understand *anything* about guilds or video games or even basic logic.

"If they were as good as Jamie," Thad said, gritting his

teeth, "one of them would have been our top healer. Do you understand that? And even Jamie wasn't good enough to compete with Red Squadron. We're up against someone who has an advantage even the *game's developers* can't get rid of. *How are we supposed to win?*"

Evan said nothing.

"Are you going to explain that to them?" Thad asked dangerously.

Evan looked at him now, and there was irritation in his eyes. He knew what Thad thought of him, clearly. He knew the team saw him as incompetent, bumbling, never authoritative enough to take a stand. They hadn't exactly made it a secret of what they thought, Thad most of all. He had no time for useless people.

Now he felt the familiar annoyance warring with disquiet. He needed Evan to help him.

"You did explain it to them," Evan said after a moment. "They did not seem to change their minds. No, I do not think I will explain it to them again."

Thad gritted his teeth. "You're just useless, aren't you?" he said, his tone falsely pleasant. "No wonder we're losing. We don't have the resources to win."

Evan did not rise to the bait. Instead, he smiled, and for the first time, Thad had the sense that maybe the other man *did* know what he was doing—and was deliberately getting under his skin.

"Nothing's ever your fault, is it?" Evan stood and gathered his folio and pen. He gave Thad a distant smile like one might give to a very insignificant underling.

Or someone who was about to be out of a job.

"*This* isn't," Thad shot back.

"Of course not," Evan said. "I'm sure it had nothing to do with you that your top healer decided to side with a rival guild over you. Just like it has nothing to do with you that you have no other healers good enough to take his place. I'm sure it's all coincidence."

He left, with Thad staring after him in quiet fury.

No one was going to help him. He saw that now. They were going to hang him out to dry and he was going to wind up as a sacrificial lamb, the first to go before they cut the program entirely.

They were going to blame him, and they wouldn't listen to someone telling them that their expectations were wrong.

If Jamie were here…

Thad's lip curled. If Jamie were here, Thad could just picture his strained expression. Jamie didn't like conflict, which was why he would never make a good leader. He shied away from disputes and wanted everyone to get along.

Thad had *thought* Jamie made a good second in command, given that he was always willing to do the tedious work of listening to people whine and calming them down.

But the more he thought about it, the more Thad realized that Jamie had always been trouble. He *said* he didn't want to lead the guild, but he had never said no when Brightstar wanted to use him for promo photos. He had never challenged Thad outright, just weaseled his way into everyone's confidence.

Lying bastard.

Thad paced around the room. They had three other

healers: Ixbal, Wentworth, and Eris.

Wentworth was out; he'd been missing his numbers for two straight weeks, and wasn't following the training program.

That left Ixbal and Eris, both of whom had clearly been at the top of their respective guilds before, and who had failed to show the reaction times and strategic thinking necessary to be the primary healer. When shit went sideways, Jamie had always been able to prioritize effectively. The other two, not so much. They had relied on Jamie's judgment in order to structure their own responses.

Frankly, Thad didn't think either of them had it in him.

He left the conference room and took the back stairs to his bedroom, not wanting the rest of the guild to see him. They were all feigning concern lately, trying to placate him, and it only made him angrier.

In his room, he paced, dug his nails into his palm, and tried to think. He wanted to tip over the shelves, throw the chair, and scream his fury at Jamie, but he couldn't let the rest of them hear. If they found out there was blood in the water…

If he was going to make this Month First, he needed a new healer, and *fast*. Thad sat down, pulled up one of the alt accounts he used on the message boards to look at what people were saying about the Demon Syndicate, and began researching the top-rated healers. *Metamorphosis Online* had not only dungeons, but also battlegrounds where players could battle one another and, while there had always been a divide between the PvE and PvP players, he wondered if he might tempt one of them to join him.

He posted a thread to draw out reactions, titled, "Do

you ever think about going PvE?" In it, he pretended to be a PvP player who wanted to know about guilds and whether running dungeons could be any fun.

He refreshed the page a few times but knew he needed to give it time.

Time, of course, being the one thing he didn't have.

His stomach growled, and he was just thinking of going to get some lunch when an email came in. He opened it, scrolled to the FROM address, and frowned.

There was none. The email had apparently come from no one.

It was only one line: *I heard you might need a healer.*

Thad looked at his post, then at his phone. He hesitated. This could easily be one of the other guilds.

Who is this?

The reply came almost immediately. *A very, very good healer.*

Character name, server, rank, Thad sent back.

Unranked.

Thad raised an eyebrow. He didn't even bother to respond to that. No one could just assume they could waltz in without a resume and get hired.

Whoever was sending the emails seemed to sense Thad's dubiousness. *Roll a character and send me the details, and I'll log in and show you what I can do.*

Why am I rolling you a character?

They didn't bother to respond, whoever they were, and with a sigh, Thad grabbed his phone and went to the practice room. He selected one of the lesser-used practice accounts, one that didn't have any characters on it for this person to steal macros or hotbar setups, and rolled a level 1

Piskie healer. He logged in, ran the character through the starting zone, and then brought his own character to the same place before sending the login details.

The Piskie appeared again almost immediately. He looked around, nodded at Thad's character, and then paused while he seemed to be bringing up several menus and sorting through them.

The pause went on for long enough that Thad crossed his arms and sighed. "I'm not waiting all day," he informed the Piskie.

The Piskie didn't pay attention, but a moment later, the character began to pulse, light strobing around it. Thad took an instinctive step back before realizing that the pulses of light were the swirl of gold sparks that signaled a level change.

The character was rising to the top level. Thad gaped, and his eyebrows shot up when the low-level robes were replaced with brocade ones of gold and red. They clashed horribly with the Piskie's green hair, but Thad wasn't paying the slightest attention to that. This set of armor was incredibly rare. Even Jamie hadn't had all of it.

"Now," said the Piskie, putting the menus away, "do you believe I know my way around this game?"

"Holy *shit*," Thad said bluntly. "Who *are* you?"

"Not important. Do you want a new healer?" The Piskie cocked his head to the side. "Word on the street is, you lost one…to Callista."

Thad's lip curled but he managed a smile, then realized it wasn't translating into the game. "A rather expensive lesson in finding out who was loyal and who wasn't. I wish it had been DPS, but we can't be that lucky every day."

DPSs were a dime a dozen compared to healers or tanks, which meant that DPS players, even the very good ones, could be replaced relatively easily.

The Piskie chuckled.

"We do need a healer," Thad said, "but I don't know what you get out of that."

"Let me handle that," the healer said. "I'll give you a training program for your guild that I want you all to follow—tactics and formations to learn."

"I'm in charge of this guild," Thad informed him coldly.

"If you don't want me, you're welcome to try to find another healer who can do what I do." The Piskie didn't sound at all worried. "This will make your guild better. *Far* better."

Thad heaved a sigh. "Test run tonight," he said. "In two hours, we'll run through the latest content, and you'll show me what you can do. *Then* I'll think about bringing you on board and changing my training routine."

He logged out without waiting for a response.

Two thousand miles away, Harry took off his headset and smiled. Finally, he'd found a way into the game, and a team that was used to following orders.

Thad might pretend to be in charge, but he didn't have any other options than to rely on Harry now—and, in the end, when he realized he couldn't win, he would do anything to punish the people who had screwed him over. He'd destroy himself willingly if Harry just pointed him in the right direction.

In Harry's opinion, *that* was the true measure of power: how well you could make a person willingly work against their own interests.

CHAPTER NINE

"All right, I straight don't know what's coming down the pipeline, but we have to be geared up." Gracie made her way through the streets of Kithara, turning sideways by instinct to avoid collisions. There weren't any, of course, but social custom seemed to be that one still behaved as if there could be.

Gracie liked that.

"What are you thinking?" Chowder asked jokingly. "A full-on siege or just some assassins?"

Gracie reached out to thwack him. "You know what I mean."

"Mmm," Caspian said vaguely. Kevin was at work right now, but Caspian, of course, had nothing to do except be online. "Are you thinking PvE or PvP? Because if you don't know, maybe we want two sets of gear."

"Wait, what?" Gracie looked at him. "Oh, my God, the battlegrounds. I'd totally forgotten about those."

"They're not as popular," Caspian said. "Some people in

our group dabbled in them sometimes, but Thad wasn't a big fan of it because of the gear repair costs."

"People didn't handle that on their own?" Gracie asked skeptically. They had reached a plaza that served as the informal temple area for the Piskies. Most of the buildings were cleverly made so that any race could get into them, but they still had the feel of Hobbit holes.

"Thad was very...controlling." Caspian's voice was tight. From the distracted way he was clipping people as he moved, Gracie could see that he was lost in thought. "He had to manage *everything* down to the smallest detail, which meant that he had to feel like the smartest guy in the room. And he wasn't always, and he had a bad temper."

"The leader should try to be the dumbest person in the room," Gracie said emphatically. "They should be smart enough to have a good sense for when they're being bullshitted, but other than that, they should want everyone around them to be experts. For instance, if I insisted no one could be smarter than me, we wouldn't be considering player versus player."

"We have to log into battlegrounds," Chowder insisted. "They couldn't exactly ambush us there, could they?" After a moment, he added, "I suppose we have to log into dungeons, too. Never mind."

"No, it's a good point. If we know it might be a trap, why log in?" Gracie chewed her lip. They were close to the armory, where players could purchase and improve gear. "It's easy to avoid PvP. Then again, if nothing else, I think we've learned that we never know what the rules are for us."

"Bingo," Chowder said. "That's a really good point, but this is a video game."

"I'm aware of that, yes." Gracie emoted a grin at him. "What's your point?"

"I don't know." The Ocru shrugged his shoulders expressively. "I guess my point is, do you lose the crown if you *ever* die? If so, are they going to be taking hits out on you? If so, how? Otherwise, they can challenge us all day, but we don't have to accept them. See what I mean?"

"Yeah." Gracie considered as she entered the armory. It was a vaulted, high-ceilinged building that was clearly modeled on the cathedral of Notre Dame, although it wasn't quite as large. She had always wondered how something so magnificent got built in a relatively new city and resolved to look up the lore later. "I think Caspian is right, though. We *should* consider being ready on a PvP front. After all, that's what Harry has been going for."

"Pssh, what can Harry do?" Chowder waved a hand, which was a surprisingly hilarious gesture in a large, muscly Ocru. "You've gone up against him *how* many times and smashed him through the floor?"

"Mmm." Privately, Gracie wasn't as confident as Chowder was.

Yes, Harry had some fatal flaws in his reasoning. He viewed his leadership through the lens of being innately better than everyone else, which meant he alienated anyone who might have helped him. It limited his abilities in combat, where Gracie's team would stand with her.

But he *was* smart, and he knew how the game was programmed. He would able to assess her strengths and weaknesses and then set up a fight that would favor him.

She wasn't going to underestimate him.

They crowded around the vendors and began scanning through gear. Chowder had been talking for a few weeks about the gear he wanted to get to shore up the gaps in his current set, and Gracie knew it would help him with his critical hit and his block chances.

Caspian had been more reticent about his gear, so she walked over to where he was standing.

"Finding anything good?"

He looked at her, cocking his head curiously.

"You have good instincts," Gracie clarified, "and a good base of knowledge. I'm curious what you'll go for."

"You don't have opinions?" He sounded deeply skeptical.

"I *always* have opinions," Gracie retorted. "Hell, I have opinions about my roommate's office dramas, and I know zero about the people involved, so I definitely have opinions about this. But you're the healer, not me. Unless we all start wiping so often that we never get through dungeons, it's not my concern."

"I like that," Caspian said. He sighed. "Sometimes I just wanted to try new things, you know? But Thad wasn't having it."

"You can always iterate with me," Gracie assured him. "I know you won't do it unexpectedly when we have a whole dungeon riding on it. Just tell any of us that you want to go experiment and we'll be there to help. Hell, tell all of us, and we'll run whatever dungeon you want."

"I know." Caspian sighed again. "That's why I left Demon Syndicate."

Gracie bit her lip. "Are you…okay?" she asked finally.

Caspian said nothing.

"I know we're not close," Gracie told him. She felt insanely awkward now. "And I just bet it was hard to make the choice you made. I hope you have someone to talk to. I'm happy to be that person if you want."

"That's nice of you," Caspian said equally awkwardly. "I mean it; I really appreciate that. Kevin's been there for me."

Gracie relaxed. With Kevin on the job, she didn't have to worry. "Kevin's a good guy," she agreed, "and *way* too wise for his years."

"I think..." Caspian's voice trailed off.

"Yeah?"

"I think he's who I want to be when I grow up." Caspian sounded embarrassed. His character was shifting from foot to foot, shoulders hunched. "That sounds so stupid."

"Nah, I totally get it." Gracie smiled. "I had a teacher like that in high school. She was the best. I just wanted to grow up and be like her. I thought she had everything figured out." She shrugged. "Now that I'm older, I think she was probably just as lost as every other adult I know, but at the time, I thought she was the coolest person ever."

Caspian laughed. "If you'd ever seen Kevin, you'd feel the same way about him. He's got this perfect apartment, and he's super in shape, and he's got a *Tesla*, and...yeah."

Gracie grinned. Caspian's hero worship was pretty adorable. "He seems like the sort of guy who wants everyone to be living their best life. I'm glad you two connected. You couldn't find a better person to live with while you get back on your feet."

She headed off to her vendor, smiling.

"Callista?" A character stood in front of her, an Aosi male with pale-greenish skin and silver hair.

Gracie stopped in her tracks. She didn't like his tone, but she didn't know what was going on, so she didn't want to be rude. "Yes?" After all, it said her name above her head.

"How does it feel to hack the game?" the character asked her. His nametag said Yaro, and he was a level 1.

Which meant he had no reason to be in the armory.

Which meant he was almost certainly someone's alt, and he was here to mess with her.

Gracie narrowed her eyes and looked him over before realizing the stupidity of that. There was no way she was going to learn about this person by studying their avatar. There were no tells in the way his mouth or his eyes moved.

"I take it you have a problem with me," she said. She kept her voice pleasant, but it took a lot of effort. *De-escalate, Gracie.*

"You hacked the rankings," Yaro said. He flashed her a smile that was clearly insincere. "You're profiting from something you didn't earn."

Gracie raised her chin slightly. "Did you explore the cave in the starting zone?"

There was a pause.

"Yes," Yaro said. He looked around as if there might be an answer to this puzzle in the stained glass windows.

"Did you see a blue jewel?" Gracie asked.

"Yes." He was sure it was a trap now, but he didn't know how to evade it.

"Did you ask the hill warden for lore?" Gracie pressed.

He said nothing.

"Did you go through an early boss fight and try to restore the balance of the non-playing factions?" She already knew the answer, but she asked it anyway. "Did you fight bosses for whom there were no guides or previews? No? Then don't tell me I hacked the rankings."

Yaro said nothing, watching her.

"You're an imposter," he said finally. "You're a hack. You're claiming to be some—*genius*—when actually you're nothing but lucky."

It touched so deeply on Gracie's fears that she instinctively wanted to lash out at him. She wanted to swing her fist and feel it connect with his jaw—

She couldn't do that. Not here, not in this world. But she *could* mute him. She could ban him. The thought came to her unbidden, so tempting that she swallowed hard against the urge to do so.

When she said nothing, it seemed to anger her opponent.

"You should leave," he told her. "You're not wanted here. You're don't deserve what you have. Other people worked harder for it."

"Who the hell do you think you are?" Caspian was at her side, making her jump. "Thad?"

"Huh?" Yaro sounded honestly confused.

"Nothing." Caspian was clearly frustrated. "Go back to your main toon, dude. Give it up."

"Fuck off," Yaro said instantly. "I'm talking to Callista, not you."

"Are you sure?" Chowder was at her other shoulder. "Because she's a member of Red Squadron, and if you mess with one of us, you mess with all of us."

"Guys," Gracie admonished. "Enough." She looked at Caspian and Chowder, meeting their eyes. To Yaro, she said, "It's clear I'm not going to say anything to win you over, so there's no point in continuing to talk, is there?"

"Maybe not for you," Yaro spat. "You can't convince me because I'm not a brainwashed idiot like those two. But you might see the truth and understand you're not welcome here. No one wants you. No one cares about you. Leave it to the pros and go home."

Gracie shrugged. "I've gotten yelled at by better people than you," she said easily. "I don't really care if you like me. There's more to this than you know, and I'm not going to bother to explain it."

Whoever Yaro was, though, he knew just how to get under her skin. Whether it was luck or some otherworldly instinct, his next words cut to the bone: "You *do* care," he said venomously. "That's why you're here, isn't it? Because everyone in your real life rejected you. Because they knew you were a piece of shit."

With any other insult, Gracie's mind would have been churning, finding retorts easily and discarding the broken logic. *Is that why you're here too?* But with this, all she could do was stand frozen, her hands twitching toward the buttons that could ban this character.

They would ban the whole account. She was sure of that.

Harry didn't do things by halves.

Do you even know how insignificant you are? The words were on the tip of her tongue as she stared him down.

"He's not worth it," Caspian said tightly. "Seriously, that's word for word out of the troll playbook. Come on."

Gracie had thought Yaro would follow them, but he didn't—and somehow that made it worse. He stood and watched as they left, and when she met his eyes one last time, her fingers twitched again to open the menu and ban him.

You're nothing, she thought contemptuously. And then, with a chill, she understood. Harry had always had this power over people.

He had always viewed them this way.

If she wasn't careful, she would, too.

CHAPTER TEN

Gracie knew that if she allowed herself to sit and stew over her confrontation with Yaro, she would work her mind into knots.

She wasn't Harry. She didn't have to *be* Harry. If her new powers were truly going to corrupt her, she would find a way to give them up (although she had the sneaking suspicion that if she were to abandon this character and roll an alt, they would show up there as well).

In the meantime, she needed to distract herself.

"Want to run one of the battlegrounds?" she asked Caspian and Chowder. "Get a feel for what we might be looking at?"

"Sounds good." Caspian created a party. "Which one do you want to do?"

"I don't know." Gracie considered, looking around at the markets of Kithara. She purposely kept herself from searching for Yaro's face in the sparse crowd and instead looked at the sky, where birds were circling and a few clouds scudded lazily. She looked back at Caspian. "You said you've run some of them, right? You queue us."

"Right." Caspian sounded a bit nervous, and she guessed that in his old guild, he wouldn't have been allowed to make many choices for himself.

Part of her still wanted to mistrust him, knowing that he had left the other guild behind—but a larger part of her saw that she was just worried about the new landscape of the game. Caspian had done nothing but aid them, and when push came to shove, he hadn't sold them out or hurt them. Instead, he'd made the honest choice.

And he had come here because Red Squadron had something Demon Syndicate didn't: camaraderie. If he hadn't crashed with Kevin, she was sure someone else in the guild would have offered him a place.

A moment later, there was a *bloop* and a picture flashed up on the screen: a crumbling castle made of golden stone, built next to a small lake and grown through with brilliant green trees. The text on the screen announced it as **SALADIN'S KEEP**.

"That was—" Gracie began, but they were yanked through the ether the next moment. When the world cleared again, it was so bright that she squinted out of reflex. "That was fast," she finished faintly.

"Queueing with a healer and a tank?" Caspian asked, sounding amused. "Yeah. Yeah, that's a quick way to get into a battleground."

Gracie laughed.

"What am I, chopped liver?" Chowder said, sounding aggrieved.

"Pretty much," Caspian said cheerfully. A moment later he added, "You know I'm joking, right?"

"Yeah." Chowder was laughing. "Don't worry so much, kid. We all give each other shit around here."

"Less shit-talking, more preparing," Gracie said. Huge numbers had appeared in the center of the screen, counting down from thirty. "Cas, can you give us a quick idea of what we're doing, here?"

"Oh, right." Caspian pointed behind Gracie. A flag fluttered there, bright purple with a white sigil of a lion rampant. "That's our flag. The other team also has a flag, so capture the flag, basically. There are two main groups you need: defense on the flag here, which might include someone stealthed or a tank—anyone who can keep people from getting very far—and then offense, which will grab the opposing team's flag and bring it back here while protecting the flag carrier. If they die, the flag goes back automatically."

"Who's on D?" asked someone named Jinx.

Gracie looked at her teammates, who nodded. "Caspian, Chowder, and I will stay here," she said.

"Healer comes O," Jinx said at once. Gracie could see the character now, a Piskie rogue who was geared up like crazy in a set of armor Gracie had never seen.

"Makes sense," Caspian agreed. Privately, to Gracie and Chowder, he added, "Let me know if you have questions, okay? And don't worry too much about people getting intense. You're learning, and they can just deal with it."

Gracie smiled and murmured a thank you, but all she could think was that Caspian didn't know her very well yet. None of these people was going to get more intense about winning—and more annoyed with her if she screwed up—than she herself would.

START announced the game, and the offensive group took off out the newly-opened door on one side, and over the ruined, tumbled-down wall on the other.

"We should hide," Chowder said.

"Good idea." Gracie looked around, marveling at the shift from dungeon to battleground. In dungeons, you knew that the boss wasn't going to notice you unless you got within a certain range. Patrols would cheerfully walk past the bodies of their dead comrades without noticing a thing.

Humans, meanwhile, were smarter.

This room must have been a great hall of some sort. The walls and ceiling were nearly destroyed, with just enough left to suggest how it had looked with a vaulted ceiling and tall, open windows. Carved wooden screens had fallen into the room, lying among the stone rubble with the broken long tables. If there had ever been cushions or curtains, they were long gone now.

The flag was on a dais at one end of the room where Gracie could only imagine a throne had stood.

"Four coming your way," Jinx said in a business-like tone. "A rogue, two summoners, and a tank."

"Thanks," Gracie said. After a moment of indecision, she ran over to hide behind the remainder of a column and watched Chowder dither before darting over to stand next to the door so that he could attack the other team once they arrived.

A moment later, the six opponents streamed through the door. The two summoners were Aosi, so alike they might have been twins, while the rogue was, incongruously, an Ocru, and the tank was a Piskie.

Gracie snickered at that. There was something awesome about a shin-high tank.

Chowder wasted no time going for the summoners. They had the least armor, and when he took them down, he'd take out their pets as well. Gracie approved of that strategy, and she let him handle it while she kept her eye on the rogue and the tank.

They left the summoners behind and sprinted for the flag, and Gracie timed their approach, holding herself still. Not yet, not yet, not yet—

She burst out of hiding and charged for the flag, slamming her hand down automatically in what was usually her opening move.

Which was completely useless with human players.

Idiot! She wasted a split second berating herself before getting off a stun on the tank, but she'd taken her eye off the rogue, and a moment later, a strike hit her in the back and a green haze appeared over her screen. The rogue had used a slowing poison on her.

Gracie growled in frustration and turned to slash at the rogue, but he was already out of range again. She spun back, ready to let loose with her stun again as soon as the tank was free, but the poison made her attacks take longer, and she missed the window. Another flurry of strikes came from the rogue, and Gracie watched helplessly as the tank took off.

"Chowder! The tank!"

Chowder called an affirmation and Gracie wavered for

a critical moment, trying to decide whether to attack the rogue back or head after the party.

She made the wrong choice. The rogue's poisons were stacking, reinforcing one another, and because she hadn't used her stuns, they'd had the opportunity to chain together some devastating combos. Her screen took on a red hue when her health dipped to ten percent, and with a couple more strikes, she was dead.

She resurrected in a nearby graveyard a moment later, cursing and at half-health, only to have the rogue appear a moment later and kill her again.

"Fucking hell!"

This time there was a thirty-second timer on her resurrection, and she swore quietly and inventively to herself about the rogue's maternal lineage and her own stupidity until she resurrected.

There wasn't much time left, but she put her character into a sprint and set off across the battleground at high speed. This was complicated by the fact that she wasn't entirely sure where she was going, but she could see a large group of people on the other side of the ornamental lake, so she headed for that.

It was an all-out brawl over the two flag carriers. Gracie's team had also managed to capture the flag but hadn't gotten very far. Both flag carriers were doing their best to stay alive and fight off their opponents while summoners and healers stood on the sidelines and threw desperate spells, and a third group tried to cut down the various magic wielders to take out the backup.

Gracie was close when the enemy flag carrier broke away from the group and sprinted toward the keep. She planted her feet and whipped her arm around to throw her shield, *just* in range, and was glad to see the Piskie stumble.

Ha. I can do this after all. She pelted after them, dodging around the AoE spells flickering through the melee, and was able to land a stun on the rogue who had killed her twice.

"Payback, bitch."

She kept running, her attention focused on the flag carrier. He was sprinting again, having gotten past the slowing part of her shield bash, and the enemy DPS closed ranks the next moment, all of them piling on Gracie at once.

Her team tried, they really did. A frost mage threw down an AoE rain of ice to slow the flag carrier, and their rogues took off to dart through the DPS and try to get to the flag carrier.

It was too late, however. The Piskie broke away and sprinted into the other headquarters, and a moment later, red letters appeared on the screen: **DEFEAT**.

Gracie swore, and although the battleground had a minute before it closed down, Caspian took them out of it immediately. They appeared back in Kithara with Gracie's gear damaged and her blood pressure higher than was strictly healthy.

"I made so many mistakes," she spat finally. "I used stupid *threat* strikes, I didn't pay attention to the rogue, I—"

"Yeah," Caspian interrupted. "Almost like it's a whole new set of skills, huh?"

Gracie bit off her words and closed her mouth. A moment later, she mumbled, "Hmph."

"Uh-huh," Caspian said almost smugly. "You're going to

learn the layout, you're going to develop instincts for PvP, and you're going to reset your hotbar and maybe your talent tree. But it's not going to happen on the first battleground."

"I don't like that," Gracie said grumpily.

"Really? You seemed so at peace with it." Caspian was clearly trying to keep from laughing. "Look, I'm gonna get myself some lunch. I'll be back for more battlegrounds later."

Gracie waved him off with a smile emote and logged out after a brief chat with Chowder. She knew rationally that she would get better at PvP as time went on. The thing was, a tank was not well suited to PvP, and she was almost certain Harry would make use of that fact.

She was going to have to get better *fast*.

CHAPTER ELEVEN

If he were honest, Thad had created the Piskie healer as a middle finger to the guy who was messing with him. Men who came into this game tended to go one of two ways: either their characters were big and brawny, or they were women who were attractive in an unearthly sort of way.

They didn't generally want to be Piskies with crazy hair.

The new healer, however, made no mention of it whatsoever. He—Thad was fairly sure it was a he—worked efficiently, barking orders at the various guild members as they went through the first boss.

"Who *is* this guy?" Grok asked Thad privately. "He's not ranked. Like, at *all.*"

Thad looked at him. Grok tended to think along the same lines Thad did, which could be useful—but not right now, when it meant that Grok was asking questions Thad really didn't want asked.

He didn't have a choice, after all. They were not going

to make it through the top-tier dungeons without a good healer, and neither Ixbal nor Eris was up to the task.

"He must have some skills, or he wouldn't have that armor, right?" Hopefully, his voice sounded casual. "And it's going well so far. I figured we could take thirty minutes to give him a job interview."

"Fair." Grok shrugged. "He sure likes to give orders, though."

"Yeah." Thad wanted to say that they'd talk about that, but he honestly wasn't sure they would. He needed this guy, and if that meant letting him call the shots in dungeons…

This was a nightmare. He could feel his position in the guild slipping, and it seemed like everything he did to make it better in one aspect made it worse in another. He needed a more solid team, and this healer was the missing piece?

But if the Brightstar execs got word that someone else was running the show, who was to say they wouldn't just take this new player instead of Thad?

He swallowed his fear. *Just focus on right now. Just get through the month with a healer, then figure out the rest of it.*

They were approaching the final boss now, walking across the void, and Thad felt a ripple of disquiet. The first time they had been here, they'd been racing the clock, already thrown into disarray by an unexpected first boss, not sure if their inside information had been at all good. Thad had believed they were walking into a trap.

And the time after that, they had just found out that they didn't have a gear advantage anymore.

Thad, who prided himself on being a rational person,

was still inclined to hate this place. There was something cursed about it for his guild. Then again, he supposed that maybe this was the stroke of luck they needed—a new healer, instead of one who was going to waltz off to join their enemy at the first opportunity.

The final boss waited beyond the line of pale fire on the ground. His axe hung heavy in one hand, and his eyes were pits of darkness. His armor seemed to burn from within. Thad had a vague idea that this was some figure in the lore from way back, but he didn't know more than that.

What with the craziness lately, it wasn't like he'd had time to do things like watch cinematics.

"Ready check," the new healer said.

The team looked at Thad.

"Initiate it," he said, nodding at the healer. He still didn't know the guy's name; he got cagey whenever it came up.

People checked in quickly, and they stepped over the line into the arena. A timer came up at the bottom of the screen, telling them how long it would be until the room was locked, and the main timer at the top showed their overall time left to beat the dungeon. They were doing well, even better than they had done before.

Thad waited for a frost aura from Harkness, their lead ice mage, then charged the boss. He knew the boss was bringing his axe up for a heavy downward stroke, but Thad could get under the swing in time to get behind his opponent.

After the strike, the boss pivoted to face him and Thad began building threat. The motions were as natural to him now as breathing. He held his shield up as he turned and slashed, dancing in and out to avoid the boss's heavy, slow movements. There was a tradeoff here: the slow strike timer meant that Thad had a lot of time between needing to dodge, but if he misjudged, he was a goner.

And in this particular dungeon, there was no battle resurrection. When you died, you died.

They couldn't afford for that to happen to him.

It wasn't long before the first geysers appeared, flames shooting up through the floor and coalescing into fiery ghosts. They screamed as they ran for the mages, and Thad turned to follow them.

"Stay with the boss," the new healer barked.

Thad froze and nearly missed dodging an axe swing.

That axe looked amazingly useful. Tanks could wield axes, of course, but a proper battle axe meant he'd be giving up his shield, and there was no way to do that and tank effectively. He sometimes wondered why they'd even bothered to put the mechanic in the game.

His blood was heating with anger, and he opened a private channel to the healer. "I'm the guild leader, not you."

There was a pause while the player performed a chain-heal, and then he responded acerbically, "We both know the skills I have. You can either play by my rules, and I will lend you those skills for your purposes," it was clear just how little he thought of those purposes, "or you can continue to bicker over petty indicators of rank, and I will leave."

Thad ground his teeth. He had been involved enough with the healer's words that he had missed a few strikes, and his threat was dropping. He increased it, anger lending emphasis to his movements.

"Good," the healer said, still privately. "If you do your job, I won't have to give orders where everyone can hear them."

White-hot fury washed over Thad, but he could see the team's health bars along the side of the screen, all in a safe range. Despite the boss's fire ghosts, this healer was keeping people alive.

By this time in their other attempts, things had already been going to shit—even with Jamie.

"What's your name?" Thad said. "We have to call you something."

"Perhaps you should have picked a better name than TrialHealer," the man said. "You can call me Yesuan."

"Like the dungeon?" Thad felt a flicker of suspicion, but it was gone as quickly as it came. There weren't words for him to name his thoughts; there weren't enough dots to connect yet.

"Like that." The healer didn't clarify further. "After this swing, get out to the edge of the room."

Thad didn't question it. The heals, he saw now, were coming fractions of a second more quickly than they should. Yesuan might or might not be a better healer, but he certainly had abilities the rest of them didn't have.

Well, if Callista could have a ranking from some stupid side quest, he could damned well have a healer who had a better casting time.

He dodged out and looked back over his shoulder to see the boss stomp his foot and then spin in a heavy circle, his axe out. Anyone there, Thad guessed, would have been stunned and then one-shotted by the hit.

"Back in," Yesuan said, sounding almost bored.

It *did* feel boring this way, Thad thought. There was no element of surprise and no thought that they would fail. After everything he had seen of Yesuan, there was no doubt that they would win this fight. How could they not? Yesuan could see things no one else could, level up instantly, equip himself with gear that should take months to get, and heal faster than anyone else.

So it wasn't a surprise to watch the boss's health creep down. Thad was barely checked in as he followed Yesuan's suggestions of when to get close or seek shelter. He let his mages deal with the various waves of fire ghosts and kept threat.

The boss went down, thudding to his knees and then bursting into a scatter of embers across the floor. Thad stared at them and tried to feel proud. Tried to feel anything.

The only thing he felt was the sinking sensation that he was in over his head.

They divided the loot—a few pieces had dropped, one of which would fit Yesuan, although he clearly had no need for it—and logged out, and Yesuan sent a party invite to Thad without any further explanation.

He insisted upon meeting in the ruined temple near Kithara, for some reason, the one on a hill overlooking the city. Thad climbed the slope alone, swearing internally rather than even muttering the words, and found the Piskie staring out at the world. He looked over his shoulder as Thad approached and wordlessly looked back at the view.

"So," Thad said tightly. Bitterly, he added, "You could have one-shotted that boss, couldn't you?"

"In a live-streamed Month First, that would be noticed by a great number of people." Yesuan still sounded bored. "You wanted a raid healer, and that was what you got."

Thad swallowed his anger. "What do *you* want?" He had to ask the question.

"I'll be sending you training for the rest of the team," the Piskie said. It should have been ridiculous, hearing those flat orders through the high-pitched voice filters, but it wasn't. The aura of command came through anyway. "I expect you to do that instead of your regular training."

"I would need to submit documentation to our bosses—"

"Then submit it."

Thad's hands clenched. "Fine," he said flatly. "Anything else?"

Yesuan looked at him, a long look in which Thad sensed not so much contempt as a deep and abiding disinterest. Yesuan didn't care about him at all.

"I am giving you everything you want," Yesuan said, "and you hate me for it. I should expect that by now," he added.

"Who *are* you?" Thad demanded again. His voice was tight. "Who the hell—"

"This is the path I chose," Yesuan said, clearly to himself. He brought one hand up to his mouth in a pensive gesture that would be better suited to literally any other race than a Piskie. He looked at Thad. "There is only one question I have for you: will you do what I tell you?"

Thad swallowed.

The silence stretched. If Thad had hoped to win this standoff, he wasn't going to.

"Yes," he gritted out.

"Then you will get what you asked for in return," Yesuan said. "There is nothing more to discuss. You may go."

He turned back to the view and dissolved the party, leaving Thad staring at his back for a long moment before he turned and left, hatred and fear swirling inside him—along with a growing sense of being utterly trapped.

CHAPTER TWELVE

Kevin stopped dead when he got to the apartment that night. "What am I smelling?"

"Food?" Jamie called back cautiously. "Does it not smell good?"

"No, it smells amazing." Kevin came around the corner into the kitchen. "It also smells like...yep, you're cooking it."

"My father once told me," Jamie said, concentrating for a moment as he flipped the grilled cheese sandwich, "that if you learned to cook, you'd always be able to have what you wanted for dinner. It seemed like solid advice."

"Okay, but explain how you got grilled cheese to smell *that* good." Kevin walked over and peered into the pan. "Did you sacrifice a virgin or something?"

"Well, obviously. But aside from that, the trick is pretty simple: first step, caramelize some onions in butter, then add a bit of red-wine vinegar. I don't mean half-assed caramelize them either; I mean take the time and do it right."

"Let's pretend I know what that means," Kevin said drily. He opened the fridge and peered inside. "Beer? Wine? Are you old enough to drink? I should have thought to ask last night."

"I'm thirty-two," Jamie said, aggrieved.

"You're shitting me. Well, then, beer, wine, neither?"

"Wine, I think." Jamie went back to cooking. "Where was I? Right. First, you caramelize the onions, then you sauté up some garlic in butter and mix the garlic in with the onions, then you make a mix of cheese—throw in something like gouda or gruyere—and make the sandwiches. With more butter. The key is butter."

"Aaaaand there go my abs," Kevin said, staring into the pan with resignation. "It smells good enough that I can't say I mind too much, though." He sighed deeply as he turned back to pour two glasses of white wine. "Besides which, it's not like the abs have been working out for me." He held a glass out to Jamie.

Jamie took it gingerly. "Oh God, you have actual wine glasses. I just drink wine out of…"

"Juice glasses?" Kevin said, raising an eyebrow as he took a sip.

"Definitely not straight from the bottle, I can tell you that much."

"Dear God, man. All right, we're going to teach you some things. First of all, how to pair wine with food." Kevin began taking down plates and silverware. As he set the table, he called over his shoulder, "With a melted cheese sandwich, you generally want to go with a dry wine rather than a sweet one. Something crisp. The most common kind you'll be able to find almost anywhere would be a dry riesling, but Chablis is also an option. Be careful with reds. Go light-bodied if you really want one."

"I have no idea what that means," Jamie said bluntly.

"All right, hang on." Kevin set the plates down. "You serve those, and I'm going to go get a sweeter white. I'll be right back."

"Eh?" Jamie plated the sandwiches and brought them over to the table while Kevin poured more wine—just a touch this time—and put it beside the full glass.

"Okay." Kevin sat down. "We're going to skip the minutiae of tasting wine. For now, take a bite of your grilled cheese—oh *fuck*, that's good—and then a sip of the first wine I poured you."

Jamie complied. "Okay."

"Right, now take another bite of grilled cheese—seriously, I want to marry this thing—and a sip of the other wine."

Jamie took a sip, a bit bemused, and made a face. What he'd expected to be a sweet wine tasted very sour and odd.

"Yep." Kevin smiled. "You don't have to know fancy words or anything; just read up on what types of wines go with the stuff you cook. Here, how about this: you give me some advance notice of what you're cooking for dinner, and I'll get a pretty easy-to-find wine that pairs well with it. Sound good?" He held up his glass to clink.

"Yes," Jamie said. He clinked his glass with Kevin's, took a sip, and resisted spitting the wine back into the glass. "Wrong one."

Kevin snorted quietly into his glass. "Seriously, thank you for dinner. You absolutely *do not* have to cook or anything. You're a guest."

"Who crashed here on very short notice, with you taking PTO to come pick me up at the airport during rush hour," Jamie said with feeling. He considered. "Maybe it's not a big deal to you, but it means a lot to me."

Kevin blinked at him. Jamie saw the urge to say something flippant, then Kevin smiled back. "Of course," he said simply.

Jamie went back to his food. "I can teach you how to make this," he added around a mouthful of grilled cheese.

Kevin nodded through his own bite. "I'd like that," he said after he had swallowed. He spun his glass of wine on its base thoughtfully. "Changing things up seems like a good idea." When he saw the look on Jamie's face, he added, "I'm sorry. You hardly need to be listening to me bitch about my life."

"I don't mind." Jamie honestly didn't. "I just don't…get it. You've got the car, the apartment, the clothes, you're in fucking awesome shape, and you know all that shit about how to pair wine with food. I guess I'm confused about what you think you're doing wrong." He waved his hands. "Like, you're not even an ass about knowing how to pair wine with food!"

Kevin, who'd been taking a sip of wine, choked, then wiped his mouth. "Well, thank you for that. I'm glad to know I'm not an insufferable douche."

"I didn't mean—"

"I'm just givin' you a hard time." He grinned and took another drink, then leaned back in his chair with a sigh. "Look, it's hard to explain, and not really something you'd want to hear."

"Try me." Jamie raised an eyebrow in imitation of Kevin's earlier expression.

Kevin blinked at him. "All right, then. I was supposed to be the golden boy." He shrugged. "I played baseball. I played football. I got straight As. My parents thought they knew where I was going, and that mental image was me with a career and a wife and a bunch of blond kids. And then I came out to them, and…they didn't cope with it well. Over the past couple of months, I've realized that I've spent the past fifteen years trying to be successful enough for them to be proud of me anyway." He gave a little laugh. "Goddamned stupid."

Jamie couldn't say anything for a moment. He hadn't realized until Kevin said that how similar their childhoods had been. Jamie, too, had been the golden boy, the one with the bright future.

And while he hadn't been as successful as Kevin, he'd also been the one who didn't fit into the box his parents had built for him.

He held up a finger, went to get the bottle of wine, and topped off both their glasses before holding his out. "From one embarrassment to another? I get it. I went the other way, and it didn't do me any better."

Kevin's smile was slow, and he nodded before toasting. He took another bite of his grilled cheese and sighed happily. "*Damn*, this is good. Okay, so tell me…what's going on with the guild?"

Gracie was hunched over the counter, halfway through a

stack of PB&J sandwiches, when the door opened and Alex came in with a bag of takeout. He blinked at her sandwiches, she blinked at his bag, and then he offered her a wicked smile and said, "Well, I guess I get your share, then."

Gracie gave him a pained look.

"Just kidding." He put the bag on the counter and shrugged out of his coat. "I know better than to try that. That's how a man gets killed in his sleep."

"A girl has no roommate," Gracie said philosophically before pulling out plates and forks. "Not out with Sydney tonight?"

"Meeting up with her after her shift," Alex explained. "By the way, they had a special on an insanely spicy Pad Thai, so I got you that."

"You're a dream." Gracie looked through the boxes. "I'm guessing it's this one, with the pepper and three exclamation marks drawn on the top?"

"Sounds right." Alex slid into his chair. "I'll just…sit at the other end of the table."

"Pansy," Gracie said affectionately. She opened her container carefully as Alex dug into his red curry.

"So, how's Jay?" Alex asked. "Yeah, don't touch that stuff with your bare hands."

"Not planning on it. You only gotta rub your eyes once before learning to be more careful about your life choices." Gracie took a bite. "Oh, son of a *bitch*. Holy fuck. I'm going to die. This is so good."

"Your decision-making is fucked," Alex told her. "I just want you to know that."

"Such exquisite pain, though." Gracie chewed. "It burns. Yeah, that's the stuff. Okay. What were we talking about?

Right, Jay." She grinned and shrugged. "He's good. We're good. Things are good. Except I suck at PvP...but he wasn't there to see that, so at least I don't have to run away and hide in shame."

"You suck at PvP?" Alex asked doubtfully. "*You?*"

"I'm good at *puzzles*," Gracie said, sucking in air desperately around a burning mouthful of food. "And I know the sorts of *puzzles* people set up. But fighting the people instead? That's unpredictable. People would just wait and kill you when you rezzed."

"Ah, yeah, camping."

"What *is* that?"

"It's...staying by someone's corpse and killing them when they respawn." Alex shrugged. "Staple of PvP, really. Also, you should get some water. You don't look so good."

"I'm fine," Gracie managed. "I just have to keep eating so the spice doesn't catch up with me."

"Sounds like drug addiction, but okay." Alex took another bite. "By the way, I did an unethical thing."

"You'd be great in sales."

"I know, right?" He grinned. "Harry didn't show up for his next appointment, so I looked up the address we had for him and went by. It didn't look like anyone was there, and while I was waiting, the landlord showed up and asked me if I was there for the tour. Said the guy moved out with no notice, so no idea, but…"

"Maybe he gave you a fake address." Gracie shrugged.

"No, he described the dude. Anyway, thought you'd want to know you don't have to worry about him showing up."

Gracie smiled. "Thanks." She yawned. "Why am I tired?"

"Because you have no regular schedule anymore." Alex pointed his fork at her.

"Oh, right. That." She yawned again. "So where are you and Sydney going tonight?"

Alex coughed. "We're not precisely…going *out*."

"Going down?" Gracie asked smoothly, and gave a fist pump when Alex choked on his curry. "Nailed it."

"I'll get you back for that. And anyway, I do have some time to play a bit of *Metamorphosis* before I leave. I'm jonesing."

"Yeah, it must have been difficult for you," Gracie said. "Bet the sex makes it easier, though."

Alex gave a thoughtful nod. "Well, when you put it that way… So, we gonna go do some questing?"

"Sounds good. We might catch Caspian and Kevin as well." Gracie sat back for a moment to assess the burning in her mouth. "Let me just drink about eight glasses of water, and then I'll join you." Her phone dinged and she picked it up, already grinning at the thought of a text from Jay.

Her smile died.

Alex, who had been heading back to the kitchen, stopped. "What's wrong?"

Gracie stared at the email, not answering.

You are nothing. You will be nothing. All of this will collapse around you. Yaro

CHAPTER THIRTEEN

By the time Jay logged on, almost everyone else was online. "Sorry I'm late, everyone. Just got in."

"What took you so long?" Alex asked affectionately.

"Ah, Gary Swiftbolt, old friend." Jay limbered up, running through some cursory wrist and neck rotations. He would normally do this before he logged in so that his character wouldn't appear to be having an awkward one-person dance party, but he'd been so busy today that he had eaten in the car while driving between errands. "It turns out I am employed once more, so I must do all of the stupid boring shit I won't be able to do during the day now. For everyone's information, I had a cavity, it's been four hours since the Novocain, and I still can't drink water without dribbling out the right side of my mouth."

"Pics or it didn't happen," Chowder said at once.

"Do you want some time to eat?" Gracie asked. "Or… shove food in the left side of your mouth? No soup."

"Nah." Jay accepted a party invite and started into the crush of people on the streets of Kithara. The group was all gathered in one of the parks near the edge of town. Oddly, near the NPCs that manned the PvP queues. Jay headed that way with a curious smile.

"Are you sure, man?" Ushanas spoke in his usual lazy drawl. "We can spend another five minutes hopping around a park. It really isn't any trouble."

"I've shoved about twice my usual food intake into me in the form of burgers and milkshakes, so I'm good." Jay bounced on his feet and grimaced. "And *wow*, do I need to work it off. Like a pile of lead, I tell ya."

"You should have had *my* dinner," Kevin said smugly. "Our Caspian makes the best grilled cheese sandwiches I've ever had in my life."

"He's saying that after a bottle of wine," Caspian said in a stage whisper, "so take it with a grain of salt."

"Hey, now, I also said that when I was sober." Jay could see them now. Kevin's Piskie summoner was dancing crazily on top of a fountain, and several of the rest of them had joined up around the edge of it to dance as well.

"You look like you're summoning demons," Jay told them.

"What makes you think we aren't?" Kevin waved him over. "Get in on the fun! Help us summon a bigger demon."

Jay looked at Gracie, who gave an expressive shrug. She was wearing her axe now instead of her sword. "I figure what they do while we're queued is their business." She pointed sternly at them. "But *you* are responsible for what that demon does in the keep, do you hear me? You walk it. You feed it. You clean up after it."

"We're running Saladin's Keep?" Jay asked curiously.

"Heck, yeah," Gracie said. "Also, we're going to lose spectacularly."

"I think you're underestimating yourself." Jay emoted a smile as he strolled closer. Knowing that Callista's face was modeled on her own made him feel like they were really standing in the park.

"No, I mean it. We're going to lose on purpose. Well, we're going to not-win on purpose." She waved her hands. "These are exploratory runs. We're all learning every nook and cranny of the keep, *then* we'll focus on the PvP part of it."

"Interesting." Jay bounced on his feet. "I've actually never run any of the PvP content since the world was launched. We had inter-team competitions there at one of the Christmas parties back in the day, though. I think I remember it fairly well."

The world disappeared around him and resolved a few moments later into the opening area of the Keep. They were at the northern end of the map, the ruins of a library with the traditional diamond-shaped bookshelves that Jay had seen in images of Ancient Greek and Egyptian libraries. Once, the place would have been filled with scrolls, but now there was very little left, and the wood, ivory, and metal centers of the scrolls lay strewn across the floor.

Their flag was bright green with a spinning wheel, and it stood in a shaft of light at the end of the room, silhouetted against the desert.

"All right, everyone know their part?" Gracie asked. "We leave one or two people here to hamstring their offense and give us more time, and the rest of us spread out and start exploring."

"I've done a lot of PvP, actually," Dathok said. "I'll stay and do D."

"I'll stay with him for now," Freon said. "Between a rogue and a frost mage, we should be able to seriously mess up some people's days."

"Solid." Gracie hefted her axe. "Red Squadron!"

"Red Squadron!" the rest of them chorused back.

"Aww, we're turning into a cult." She laughed as the doors opened. "Let's go explore!"

Jay didn't feel any guilt about sneaking off with Gracie. After all, the whole point of this exercise was to have fun, wasn't it? They weren't trying to win. He opened a private channel.

"Follow me."

"Where are we going?" Gracie followed him curiously. They were heading along the outer wall, going west, and she was looking around at everything. Once or twice, she tried to slide into gaps in the wall. "That's a good spot," she said after one of them. "Not sure what you'd use it for, but if you could sort of herd a flag carrier down this way, maybe?"

"Good call." Jay hopped onto a toppled column and ran up it.

"Where are you going?"

"Come on!" he called back.

Gracie laughed as she followed. She had put a glamor on her armor to make it a dusky, aged bronze color rather than the bright gold it had been before—very like her to do, in Jay's opinion. With the axe and darker armor, she looked a good deal more deadly.

Jay led the way up the column and onto the slanted remains of the roof that ran along a side hall. This had been one of the places the developers had held victory dance parties when they won, and it offered a gorgeous view of the desert around the keep as well as the verdant oasis inside.

Plus, on an artificial roof, there was no chance of slipping on a stray tile and crashing to earth.

From here, they could see the whole battlefield, and Jay swept his arm out triumphantly. "Behold the site of your future victory." He cleared his throat. "At some point, I assume I'll find out why we're focusing on PvP now."

"*Awesome*," Gracie breathed. "This is great, thank you. And as for the PvP…" She looked over with a shrug. "Call it a hunch."

"Mmm?" Jay watched as a series of frost spells went off in the library. "Freon and Dathok have company."

"Hamstring 'em, boys," Gracie cheered. She had crossed her arms and was frowning as she surveyed the ruins of the keep.

Saladin's Keep sat at a crossroads that was no longer used; the roads stretched away, cobblestones scattered and quickly lost in the drifting sands. The building was massive and still sheltered the oasis, even in its tumbled-down state.

The two ends of the keep formed the bases for the PvP match. At one end was a dining hall, where Saladin had entertained the most distinguished of the caravan leaders, scholars, soldiers, and nobles who passed through the crossroads, and at the other end was the library. In between, were the old kitchens, bedrooms, and even a temple. Outside the walls of the keep proper were longer, lower walls where caravans would have camped.

In the center was the most innately interesting feature of the keep: the oasis. Possessing a large pool of clear, deep-blue water, it was surrounded by tall palm trees, bushes, and flowers. From the way Gracie stared at it, Jay knew that in the real world, she was lost in its beauty, even if he couldn't see it on her avatar's face.

"What are you thinking?" he asked her after a moment.

"I'm thinking that the oasis draws people in, but it's the most useless place," Gracie said slowly. "The rooms, the corridors, the roofs—all of those are better for a run with the flag. If you worked together as a team, you'll be able to—"

DEFEAT flashed up on the screen.

"Whoops," Gracie said. She switched to the main channel. "Anyone know if we can re-queue in here?"

"We can," Caspian said. "Because we're a full group. We're just all going to get yanked back to the starting room, and it may flip-flop us to the other one when we get opponents."

"Cool," Gracie said. She pointed to a series of rooms just below them: "Okay, so, real quick… If you look there, you can see that there are a lot of ways through the—dammit!" The reset had yanked them back to the main room. "Blast."

"Yeah," Jay said. "No, I see what you meant. Next time, let's…"

"Let's?" Gracie looked at him.

He made sure he was on the private channel before answering. "Well, what I *should* say is that we should take everyone to get acquainted with the path so we can try things out, but what I actually wanted was to spend some time with you."

"So let's do that," Gracie said with a smile emote. She gave him a thumbs-up. "We can lose at this any day of the week, man."

Jay burst out laughing.

"All right," Gracie said to the group. "We have a hunch that the best way to run this is to go down the side corridors instead of through the oasis, no matter how pretty it is and how it seems like the best place to go. There aren't many places to hide backup, and it's just a clusterfuck. If we make a team effort to go down one of the sides, though, we're in good shape. Jay and I will take the west side and note anything we see there, Ushanas and Fys, take the east side to see about ranges for AoE and pets, and the rest of you work on various defensive hiding places or offensive tactics. Try range, try sneaking up on people, try anything you want."

"Roger that," Dathok said. "Freon and I are still on defense, I assume?"

"Yep," Gracie responded. She clapped for the two of them. "Everyone, say thank you to Dathok and Freon for giving us the space to try this out."

"Thank you," the group chorused, sounding like a group of five-year-olds.

The countdown began again, and Gracie and Jay ran over to the west side of the library. She held up her hand for an e-fist-bump and he tapped it before the barriers disappeared and they took off.

They raced one another, hopping over tumbled stones and ducking under barriers. He heard a laugh, and he looked over to see Gracie stumble.

"I actually *jumped*," she said, amused, "rather than using the controls. Not great on the landing. My downstairs neighbors probably hate me."

Jay laughed. They were in the long gallery of the temple, which was set up with what looked like altars to many gods. That would make sense in a place like this, he supposed. Most of the statues were gone, however, or destroyed.

He wondered what had happened here.

They moved through more slowly now, practicing hiding behind statues or in alcoves. None of the other team seemed to be coming this way.

"So, why are we doing PvP now?" Jay asked her.

She looked at him seriously, her hair drifting around her face in an unseen wind. "I think it's how Harry will come for me next time."

"*Can* he?" Jay asked skeptically. "He had to inhabit bosses last time. He wasn't able to start the quest himself. Unless…can he port a boss in here?"

"I don't think so," Gracie said. "But there are a million ways he could set me up to fail. He knows the rules of this game, Jay, and I don't. The *real* game, I mean, not *Metamorphosis Online*. *His* game."

"Good point." Jay crossed his arms and sighed as he considered. "I wish I knew what to tell you," he said finally. "I don't know much about PvP."

"I suck at it," Gracie said. "People do the stupidest things just to be spiteful, so it's not like fighting a computer where it's set up to make you do things that are legitimately difficult. No, you have to account for the fact that people might make a stupid decision just to fuck you over. I hate it."

Jay smiled at her.

"What?" She crossed her arms.

"Are you sure you haven't been replaced with a pod person?" Jay asked her. "Because the Gracie I know really, really likes winning, and she sure doesn't back away from a fight."

Gracie snorted, annoyed. "I like winning fights that are *worth* winning," she said grumpily. "Not fights that are full of bad logic."

"Can't this one be both?" Jay asked her. "Because, yes, if we wind up fighting PvP, it will be as much a mind game as a skill game. That's true. But what we'll be fighting for… well, it's the same thing we've always been fighting for. And that's worth it."

CHAPTER FOURTEEN

It's the same thing we've always been fighting for. And that's worth it.

The thought was still circling in Jay's head when he pulled into the parking lot of Dragon Soul Productions the next day around noon. His team had gotten used to working across the entire day, focusing heavily on the evenings, when the bulk of players were online. When he'd first met Gracie, they had been in a phase of working from 8pm until 4am.

He had chosen to walk away from this place, and he would do it again—but he had missed it. Gracie had put into sharp focus all the things he loved about Dragon Soul and the game they had created. His team had worked hard to create a new home for people who needed an escape. Jay had liked being part of that, and he had liked his team.

Now he was back, and he found himself unexpectedly nervous. Not knowing what to do, not knowing what Dan and Dhruv might come after him or his coworkers for, he hadn't been in contact with any of them except Sam since he left. Several of them had texted him to ask if he was okay, but Jay hadn't written back.

Would they even be glad to see him?

When he arrived, the place was quiet. Computers hummed, but no one seemed to be around. Jay stopped, frowned, and pulled out his phone to check the start time Sam had given him.

It *did* say noon.

But maybe this had been some elaborate prank by Dan and Dhruv. No, that was ridiculous.

Right?

He was chewing his lip when Sam popped his head out the door of one of the conference rooms. "There you are. Wanted you to come in early for all the HR paperwork bullshit. Come on, I got bagels."

With a small sigh of relief, Jay headed down the hallway, swinging his messenger bag over his head. He walked into the room with a hello and jumped when a chorus of voices called, *"WELCOME BACK!"*

Jay's old team was all there. Some of them looked deeply disheveled, and all of them had donuts and caffeine in their hands. A full spread of breakfast food had been set out, and people came up to give Jay handshakes and tell them how glad they were that he was back.

Jay gave Sam a bemused smile, and his boss edged closer.

"I figured we'd do this before Dan and Dhruv were in," Sam said, his voice low. "They agreed that you could come back, of course."

"But a whole *party* might be pushing it?" Jay asked. He

nodded at Sam. "Seriously, thanks. This is awesome. I missed these guys."

"They missed you," Sam said. "Also, while you're here—Ria, Paul." He beckoned over two people who looked vaguely familiar to Jay. "You were in on first interviews for both of them."

"Oh! Right." Jay shook their hands.

Paul had long, floppy brown hair and was wearing a much-too-large polo shirt, and Ria was tiny and delicate, dark-haired, and with an aura of someone who was trying to pack far too much energy into her small frame. She was, paradoxically, the only one in the room not holding a cup of coffee or a bottle of soda.

Jay nodded at them both. "Settling in well?"

"Yeah," Ria said. "Had to hack one of the VR suits to make it fit, but we managed."

"She's a male Ocru in-game," Paul said, snickering.

"I wanted to know what it was like to be tall," Ria said as if it should be self-explanatory.

Jay laughed as they wandered off and glanced at Sam. "So? *Is* there actually any HR paperwork bullshit to do?"

"Only a couple of things." Sam waved a hand. "We can get it done anytime. Get some breakfast, since I know you don't eat much in the mornings. Saw you were doing some PvP last night."

Jay, who had been picking up a cinnamon sugar donut, raised an eyebrow.

"I still have all the controls hooked up to watch you," Sam said with a shrug. "I'd say it's safe to assume they are as well." He didn't need to say who *they* were.

"I don't suppose we could expect anything else," Jay

said, sighing. "Looking for ways to bring her back to zero, huh?"

"Jay, you know it's not that." Sam was serious now. He peered around the room. "This...isn't the place for this. Get a plate—no, a full plate, a donut is not a balanced breakfast—and we'll do the paperwork. All right, everyone, wave to Jay, you'll see him later, I have to take him to do paperwork."

Everyone groaned and waved, and Jay and Sam walked to his office in silence.

When they got there, Sam sat in his chair and took a moment to choose his words while Jay mixed sugar into his coffee.

"How's Gracie?" Sam asked finally.

"Fine." Jay gave him a look.

"I was actually asking." Sam raised an eyebrow. "It's clear you care for her." There was a question in those words.

Jay sighed and took a bite of his donut. "Yes," he said finally. "We're together. No, we've never met in person. No, I am not going to have a lecture on—"

"Did you really think I brought you back here to lecture you and threaten your girlfriend?" Sam asked him. "I think I've earned the benefit of the doubt from you."

It was a good point. Sam had risked his job multiple times to create distractions for Red Squadron and hamstring the Demon Syndicate. Not only that, he'd been a good boss in general, always putting himself in the way of employee code changes or unwarranted discipline.

"You're right. I'm sorry." Jay frowned, frustrated. "But I

don't see how you can support them. You've watched what they've been doing."

"Jay, just because I don't think it's right to have people buy their ranking in this game, that doesn't mean I'm all right with having some sort of demigod queen." Sam shook his head. "And I *definitely* don't think it's a good idea to have Harry's programming still in the game. I'm sure she's a wonderful person. I have nothing against *her*. But I want her to be a player. I want the game to be solid and secure and enduring."

Jay could think of nothing to say to this.

"They haven't said it," Sam said, "but I think part of why Dan and Dhruv wanted you back is that you seem to have better luck than they do at finding the pieces Harry left behind. Jay, you seem to think this is all over because she got what he wanted. Have you actually paid attention to any of the stories about Harry? Because he won't let it end here."

Jay's head came up. His chest felt cold and hollow. "You think he's planning something more?"

"Of *course,* I think that." Sam looked at him like he had two heads. "Don't tell me Gracie doesn't agree."

"No, she...she said she expected a PvP battle." Too late, he realized he shouldn't be talking about this with Sam. The words were out of his mouth, though, and there was no coming back from it. "I just thought she might be wrong."

"Jay, you're a very good employee," Sam said. "You're smart, you're capable...and sometimes you're a complete moron."

Jay spluttered through a sip of his coffee.

"Gracie is *right*," Sam said grimly. "Dan and Dhruv know it; anyone who knows what's going on knows it. You... I don't know what's going on with you."

"He hasn't been able to get into the game," Jay said, annoyed. "She has his powers."

"Like that's really going to be the end of it for someone that vengeful?" Sam shook his head. "This is making me worry about your relationship. Look, a few quick tips: pay attention to the things your partner likes, so you can do something fun for her birthday. When in doubt about—"

"I'm *fine* on relationships," Jay said, nettled. "*Thank you.*"

"Are you sure, man?" Sam shook his head. "Well, your funeral, I guess. Hit me up if you ever spectacularly biff a holiday."

"I am not going to... You know what? I am *not* having this discussion with you." Jay jabbed a finger at him. "I am totally aware of the situation; I just don't think it's dire."

"Then prove it," said a new voice. Dan was leaning in the doorway, his arms crossed. He nodded at Jay. "I don't suppose there are any donuts left."

"Probably," Sam said. He didn't seem worried at all.

"I'll go get one in a moment, then." Dan looked at Jay. "In the meantime, *do* know that no one would be happier than us if you were to find out there was no game-destroying kill switch. That's what you're going to be spending your time on. It could be anything. Lord only knows how he could have hidden it."

Jay considered this silently. Gracie would want him to do this, he knew, but he still had some questions. When this was over...

"Find it before Harry destroys the game," Dan told him seriously, "and we'll let Gracie stay as whatever she is. That will be the end of it."

Jay reached out to shake the man's hand without hesitation. "Deal."

CHAPTER FIFTEEN

"That was fucking weird," Kevin called from the living room.

"Eh?" Jamie stirred the pasta in the pot, then went back to the frying pan, where thick-cut bacon cut into small pieces was frying up. A small bowl of peas sat next to a heaping bowl of freshly shredded parmesan, a pinch bowl of red pepper flakes, a glass of white wine, and some egg yolks.

Kevin came around the door with his VR headset under his arm. He was still wearing the rest of the suit over a plain white t-shirt and workout pants. Jamie had come to learn that Kevin *had* no casual clothes.

They were going to fix that. Jamie believed strongly on a moral level that no gamer should go through life without a comfortable sweatshirt and a pair of flannel pants.

"PvP just takes some getting used to," Jamie told Kevin now. He checked the table to make sure he'd put out silverware. "Did you—"

"It wasn't the keep," Kevin said. He put the headset on

the counter and began stripping off the rest of the suit, still frowning. "So, I finished, and I went over to the armory, right? I wanted to find some armor that might help with interrupts, and also healing modifiers."

"Sure." Jamie tested the pasta, smiled, and used a measuring cup to scoop out some of the pasta water.

"What on earth are you doing?"

"You'll see." Jamie waved for him to continue and grabbed the potholders so he could drain the pasta. "Go on."

"I wasn't paying a ton of attention in the battleground," Kevin said, "so he might have been there or something? But this guy was definitely following me in the armory. Like, I turned around, and he was just staring at me. I figured he was AFK or something, but every time I moved, there he was."

Jamie set down the colander of pasta. He was beginning to get a very bad feeling about this. "Yaro," he said.

"Yes," Kevin said. His frown deepened. "How did you— Okay, well, who is this guy? Because he told me that Callista was a hack and said she'd drag everyone down with her and I should cut and run. Basically. But, like, super creepy?" He shuddered elaborately, which only served to show off the muscles over his whole torso.

Jamie was beginning to think that he might need to go to a gym one of these days. He'd always thought he was in pretty good shape, but Kevin looked like the sort of person who'd taken the time to figure out all of the really weird machines, and who probably talked about them casually like it was no big deal. After their PvP battles the night before, when Jamie had logged out, sweating and panting, Kevin had looked like he'd been out for an evening stroll.

It was just bad for the ego.

Jamie put the wine and red pepper into the frying pan, stirred it with the bacon, and added the pasta. He mixed it with the bacon, added some of the pasta water, added the egg yolks, and began to add the parmesan in increments. Kevin had put away his VR suit and was now watching carefully, taking note of each step. When Jamie nodded to the plates, Kevin held them out for a heaping portion of carbonara.

They brought their plates to the table in relative quiet, Kevin pouring wine, Jamie adding another spoonful of parmesan on top of each plate and putting out bread. He'd forgotten to get ingredients for a salad, he remembered now. Oops.

"So this is carbonara," Kevin said. He took an exploratory bite; his manners, as usual, were impeccable. His eyebrows shot up, however. "Damn. *Damn*."

"Really good, right?" Jamie smiled. "The trick with Italian food is a light touch. It gets very heavy if you're not careful. Also, there's a lot more to Italian food than we generally think of. Anyway, what are we drinking?"

"Pinot Grigio," Kevin said. He took a sip and nodded. "It works well. I went Italian since this is Italian food, but the French equivalent would be a Pinot Gris, and the Spanish equivalent would be a Rueda. Pinot Grigio is one of the common ones, though. Easy to find. You want something crisp."

"Yeah, I don't know what that *means*," Jamie said bluntly.

"Here's the deal." Kevin was grinning. "You go into the

wine store. You ask them for the type of wine that pairs with the dish you're making. They tell you the type, and sometimes they tell you their favorite. Try that one if they do. If they don't, you go to that section and you look for one that has a little review tag written by a wine magazine. You try that one, and if you like it, you have your Pinot Grigio or whatever. If you don't, the next time you try a different one."

"I *like* that," Jamie agreed slowly. "I can follow those instructions.

Kevin lifted his glass with a smile. "Wine is not as complicated as people think. The dirty little secret is to drink whatever the hell you want."

"I'm not sure you know what dirty little secrets are, but okay." Jamie grinned back. "I think this turned out well."

"Ridiculously well," Kevin agreed. "All right. Not to ruin the food with shop talk, but I'm still unnerved. Who the hell is Yaro?"

"Oh." Jamie blew out a breath. "He was following Gracie the other day. I don't actually know who he is. He was being just an incredible jerk to her. You know, getting on her case about being a nobody, being the sort of person who escapes into an online world because everyone in her real life knows she's a piece of shit…"

"People who live in glass houses," Kevin murmured.

"Right?" Jamie laughed, but he rubbed his forehead. "I thought he was just a troll, but if he's following you, too, it sounds like he has a grudge."

"Delightful." Kevin tugged his lip, then dipped a piece of bread in olive oil and chewed, considering. "Do you think it might be someone from your old guild? Or another guild?"

"That could easily be it," Jamie admitted. "It could be…"

Kevin raised an eyebrow as he took a bite of spaghetti. He gestured for Jamie to finish the thought.

Jamie shrugged helplessly. "It could be Thad," he said quietly. "I honestly don't know. I really don't. It might be him, or it might not."

"I don't know much about him," Kevin said. "I know he had a temper, and he must not have been a very good friend, or you wouldn't be here."

Jamie felt a pang of guilt. "He *was* a good friend."

"Was he?" Kevin looked doubtful.

"He taught me the game," Jamie said.

"Yeah, anyone can do that. Gracie and Jay helped me and Alan at the start. We helped them. Alan taught her some of the terminology. That's just called not being an ass."

"Good point." Jamie shrugged. "You know how some people *need* to be in charge? Thad's one of those. I told Gracie that. He needs to make every decision. He always chose what we ran, who was on the run, and how everyone trained. If you didn't like it, you could leave. But it's not unusual for that to happen on a competitive team," he added out of a sense of fairness. "There are a lot of strong personalities."

"Weak personalities," Kevin corrected. "That's *weak*, not strong. Was he the one who suggested sending you to sabotage us?"

Jamie laughed bitterly and ended up taking a much bigger swallow of wine than he had meant to. He got it down and took a bite of bread. "No. No, *he* wanted to be the one doing the infiltrating. Gracie would have spotted him in a hot minute. He's not very good at...being subtle."

Kevin snorted, then smiled. "Ahhhh. Someone *else* chose you."

"Yep." Jamie shrugged. "The execs at Brightstar have always liked me."

"You don't say," Kevin murmured.

Jamie frowned at him.

Kevin gave a slightly secretive smile as he took a sip of wine. "Well, for one thing, let's just say that between you and a control-freak with an oversized ego, I know who *I'd* want to spend time with."

Jamie flushed slightly. "Er. Thanks." He cleared his throat. "Anyway, yeah, they had me do the infiltrating, Thad didn't like that much, and then, well...I had a lot more fun playing with you guys than I had ever had before. It's a super cool game, don't get me wrong, but playing it was always stressful because we were trying to beat bosses and every move was measured. We'd get called out after for a time we'd gone left instead of right, or…"

Kevin looked deeply unimpressed.

"It worked," Jamie said. "We were the top guild for a while."

"And then you stopped being the top guild," Kevin said. "Because Thad was so damned unpleasant to be around that your literal enemies were more fun to hang out with."

Jamie was surprised into a laugh. He hesitated, then admitted the truth. "I didn't want to like you guys."

Kevin looked amused as he took another bite.

"Alan was a big part of it," Jamie said. He'd been curious

about Alan since he got here. He knew that Alan and Kevin lived in the same city, and someone had said they were brothers, but Jamie would never have guessed that. "Could I...meet him?"

"Oh! I meant to tell you. He was going to come over this weekend." Kevin waved a hand. "Sorry, totally blanked. He's been slammed at work, what with the semester ending and everything, but he says he does want to meet you."

"He's nice."

"He's very nice." There was no irony in Kevin's voice. "Best big brother I could ask for, although we weren't close when we were little." He saw Jamie's questioning look. "I was the favorite. It was awkward. Our parents did a pretty good job of driving a wedge between us, even though I don't think they were specifically going for that." He swirled the wine in his glass and gave a theatrical shrug. "We got a lot closer once we were *both* disappointments."

Jamie laughed. He was clearly meant to.

"But tell me about Thad." Kevin leaned forward. "Because Gracie is clearly worried something is coming, and I don't think she's focusing enough on him. This Yaro guy just unsettles me."

"It doesn't seem like the sort of thing Thad would do," Jamie said after considering it. "Like I said, he's not subtle. If he confronted her, it would be a screaming match. He wouldn't be able to keep his cool and be creepy or anything. Although..." He took another bite as he thought. He was hoping Kevin would interject, but the other man said nothing, so Jamie sighed. "I honestly don't know what Thad might do right now. I've never seen him in a situation like this."

"Like what?" Kevin raised an eyebrow.

"He...constitutionally doesn't seem to think he can lose," Jamie said. "Like, he just... Some people can't even process that possibility, right? He's one of them. He's always worried what people think of him, and he has to be the smartest one in the room, the one in control, but he also just assumes it's all going to work out."

Kevin said nothing, just leaned back in his chair, still swirling the wine in his glass.

"So what happens when he realizes he's lost?" Jamie asked. "What would he do if he thought someone had won the game so completely that he could never climb back up the rankings?"

"Lose his cool," Kevin said as if it were self-explanatory. "Have a screaming match, lose a few more guildmates—"

"I don't think that's what we should worry about," Jamie said bluntly. "I really don't."

Kevin frowned at him. He had long since finished his pasta, and now he pushed his plate aside and leaned on his forearms. "Talk to me. If you were a Sim, you'd have a little thundercloud over your head or something."

That made Jamie laugh. "Okay, here's the thing. Thad's really conscious of his reputation. If he hasn't got that, he hasn't got anything, right?"

"Right." Kevin nodded.

"So if he's lost his reputation, he has nothing else to lose," Jamie stated bluntly.

Kevin's face grew solemn. He was beginning to understand, Jamie thought.

"So you're worried that...what exactly are you worried

about? What do you think he'd do?" He sounded urgent now.

"I don't *know*." Jamie clenched his fingers instinctively, then hastily put down his wineglass before he cracked the stem. "That's the thing. I don't think he has it in him to do something like Yaro is doing—play a long game and creep people out, chip away at them, all of that. Thad's style is more...explosive. More kamikaze."

"So you think he's going to dive-bomb Red Squadron somehow," Kevin said.

"Yeah." Jamie swallowed. "I think if he finds a way to get back at Gracie, he's going to do it—no matter what the cost to him."

CHAPTER SIXTEEN

Jay stared at the database and wanted to beat his head against the desk.

When they had started this a few weeks back, he'd been filled with inspiration. He had been doing something he wasn't supposed to do: fighting against a common enemy and trying to help Gracie finish the quest he earnestly believed she was meant to finish. He'd been searching through the database, following the clues in each encounter...

And now he couldn't even think of where to start.

If he were Harry, how would he hamstring the game? Where would he put the bomb? Jay had no earthly idea.

The urge to beat his head on the desk got stronger.

He rolled his chair over to the whiteboard at the side of the room, took a marker down, and stared at the shiny surface.

Nope, that wasn't working either.

He looked around his office. This place was soulless— that was part of it. He had been in a cubicle before, but now he had an office with white walls and a plain desk and absolutely nothing to make it look like it was his. No desk toys. No pictures. Not even a pen.

That gave him an idea, though. Jay considered, then brought up the global rankings screen. It took a few clicks for him to get to where he needed to go, and he was smiling as he made some adjustments on his screen. He wasn't a graphics genius by any stretch of the imagination, but he could do basic things.

He hit Print and headed to the printer on the other side of the floor. A few people called hellos, and he waved. It was good to be back. He hadn't let himself think about how much he'd missed this place, but he really had. He'd missed his teammates, and he had genuinely enjoyed the work he did here.

The printer was almost finished by the time he got there. Jay waited, then went back to his desk and looked around for some tape and scissors. It was fairly quick work to put the picture up.

He didn't have any pictures of Gracie, after all...so a picture of Callista would have to do. He grinned at the blue-skinned face. The tank was staring imperiously out into space in her screen grab from the global rankings. You could fully believe that she was some long-lost queen, ascendant in this new world.

At some point, he'd have to get a proper picture, though.

He went back to work with a renewed sense of purpose. He took the marker, went back to the whiteboard, and began writing down what he knew about Harry.

1) Metamorphosis Online *was Harry's idea.*

Harry had come up with the world back at the start. Jay didn't know quite how that would inform things, but that was the deal about making lists like this. You didn't know what was important until later.

2) Harry believed that people should not be allowed to do whatever they wanted in-game because it would make them bad people outside the game.

Which led quickly to more points. Jay's handwriting was turning into a scrawl.

3) Dhruv believed the opposite. They fought about it, BUT—

4) Harry didn't make the quest until Dan and Dhruv booted him out?

5) Which means maybe there were failsafes built into the rest of the game already.

6) Or he had some other method of controlling things

7) Would he plan far enough ahead to account for the idea that maybe the whole game world would go "out of control" and he had to go for a nuclear option?

Jay capped the marker and sat back in his chair, crossing his arms and staring at the board, then got up to write another point down.

8) Harry wrote the Yesuan quest

That was probably important. The problem, of course, was that it meant Harry was batshit loonball insane, although it wasn't as if that was a completely new revelation. Jay scratched his head. He wished Gracie were here.

Then again, he was glad that she wasn't. She was working on the PvP, and he would be glad to come back to her with at least some idea of a solution rather than just a problem. She would have good ideas; he was sure of that. She'd always had a fairly good sense of Harry's general style—but it would be better to bring her in once Jay had gone over some preliminary thoughts.

She'd let him know if he was missing anything, he was sure of that.

He smiled slightly and shook his head, and was still staring at the board, resigned, when Dhruv came into the room. Jay jumped and stood up hastily.

"No, no, no need to stand." Dhruv waved him back into his chair and sat in the other one, looking at the board. He crossed his arms as he read. "What's the end goal of this list?"

"Trying to figure out what sort of failsafe Harry would build in, or if he thought to build one in at the start," Jay said. "I still don't even get how he made Gracie's quest, honestly."

Dhruv gave a ready grin. "He'd be so fucking mad to hear you call it *her* quest."

Jay laughed. He was still a bit unnerved to be sitting in a room with Dhruv of all people, but the Dragon Soul founder seemed to not be in a confrontational mood. Jay pointed at the board. "I think the thing is this... Harry wrote the Yesuan quest, right? So he knew that people didn't necessarily like the sort of dictator he wanted to be. He got that."

Dhruv gave a noise that somehow managed to convey both Harry's melodrama and Dhruv's dislike of it. He gestured for Jay to continue.

"But did he think it would go wrong enough that he'd need to nuke it from orbit?" Jay asked. "If so, was it meant to reboot the game, or totally kill it? Or was it something more subtle, forcing players into some sort of...re-education?"

Dhruv gave him a sort of queasy look. "That does sound like something he'd do, doesn't it? Dammit. That's disturbing."

"Or," Jay said, "did he have time to build the quest but not anything else—because he had just assumed that he would be able to be in the game with all of the moderation tools? In which case, we're in an Apollo 13 situation, and he's sitting over there trying to figure out how to destroy the game with only the tools he has at his disposal."

Dhruv gave a laugh that turned into a cough. "Honestly, I'd assume he built the game with the sort of controls he thought he would need. When he realized he wasn't going to have those, he built the quest. Which means, if we want to know how he thinks, we'll want to know what powers Callista has now."

Jay paused. For a moment, he had forgotten who he was talking to, and then he had remembered that Dhruv was not exactly his ally. When he looked over, Dhruv was looking at him shrewdly.

"Dan made you the offer," he said. "And I intend to stand by it."

Jay narrowed his eyes. "But?"

"What do you mean?" Dhruv asked easily.

"You *don't* mean to stand by it," Jay said slowly. "You have doubts."

Dhruv thought about this for a moment. "You worked here for, what, three years? You made a good salary, you had a considerable number of friends, and by all accounts, you enjoyed the work you did. Yes? And then you threw all of it away for someone you'd known for a few weeks."

Jay, not sure where this was going, kept his mouth shut.

"Why?" Dhruv asked. "What was it about her?"

Still, Jay said nothing. Saying the words to Dhruv felt like a betrayal. He wanted to speak about smiling at Gracie on the roof of Saladin's Keep, but that memory was *theirs*. It was for people who cared about both of them.

"If she's the woman you think she is," Dhruv said, "you have nothing to worry about." With that not-very-reassuring sentiment, he stood and smiled. "Ask her if she's willing to share the menus she has. You might be surprised."

Jay said nothing. He stared at the whiteboard while Dhruv left. The problem, he decided, was that you *wanted* to like Dhruv. He spoke openly, and he told you when he was angry. You knew what you were working with.

Jay got up and poked his head out into the hall. "Hey. You have another minute?"

Dhruv turned to look at him and came back with a curious smile. Jay could see the people nearby craning to get a look as subtly as they could. Jay and Dhruv were on speaking terms? Dhruv was leaving Jay's office without it being a screaming fight? What was going on?

"Talk to me about the fights," Jay said, tapping the board.

2) Harry believed that people should not be allowed to do whatever they wanted in-game because it would make them bad people outside the game.

3) Dhruv believed the opposite. They fought about it, BUT—

4) Harry didn't make the quest until Dan and Dhruv booted him out???

Dhruv's eyebrows went up. "And you want a summation that fits in...a minute, I believe you asked for?" He shrugged. "He's a douche."

Jay pressed his lips together. "Okay, I deserved that. Do you have enough time to walk me through that part, though?"

Dhruv heaved a sigh. "Yeah, I think so," he said finally. "I have a meeting with Brightstar, and it wouldn't be the worst thing in the world to let them stew a bit." He typed something quickly on his phone and shut the door to Jay's office before starting to pace.

"Harry liked me," he said finally, "for the same reason he hated me: I talked back to him."

Jay sank into his chair and watched the man pace. Dhruv was running his fingers through his dark hair, which he kept on the long side.

"When we were roommates, it was....fine." Dhruv grimaced. "I thought he was an asshole—not incorrectly—but he *was* smart and funny, and he was willing to 'try out' letting other people win arguments. By which I mean, he won and lost the same number of arguments; he just *admitted* when he lost them." He rolled his eyes and perched briefly on the arm of the second chair before springing up again to pace some more.

Apparently, Dhruv did not excel at sitting still.

"Dan was Harry's kryptonite," Dhruv continued, "because he never just comes out and *fights* you on anything, he just sort of pivots, and you end up arguing with thin air. Harry couldn't pin him down. He was stupid enough to think that was because Dan agreed with him all the time."

Dhruv shrugged. "It works for him, I guess, but I don't do things that way. Anyway, the long and short of it was that Harry always had to think of someone winning an encounter. There was the person in charge, and then there was everyone else in some sort of crab-bucket battle royale."

Jay blinked, trying to picture this.

"Harry talked a lot about *Metamorphosis* when we were in college," Dhruv explained, "but no one thought he could pull it off, and he hadn't built the whole world out. We were the ones who did the early planning and tests with him. We stress-tested his ideas. It wouldn't have been possible without us. He acknowledged that, but he still had to be in charge. He couldn't deal with someone else having a good point, definitely not in public. You could get around him sometimes. You could see him in private, and sort of talk him into agreeing with you, and then he'd pretend the idea was his." Dhruv gave a disgusted look. "Dan found that out. I did it once and... Well, I *tried* it once."

Jay, despite himself, laughed quietly. He couldn't imagine Dhruv sneaking around, trying to maneuver someone into taking credit for his idea.

"Yeah, laugh it up," Dhruv said sourly. "We had a screaming fight, and I never tried it again. My point is, Harry always had to win. Not only win but be so far ahead that no one else could come close to beating him." He finally sat, dropping gracelessly into a chair. Dhruv in motion was one thing, but at rest, he looked lanky, like a figurine with slightly wrong proportions.

Jay considered this. "Gracie said there were controls to mute people," he said, "or block them, ban them, that sort of thing."

"There we go," Dhruv said. "Now we're getting somewhere. Has she used them?"

"No." Jay looked at him like he was crazy.

Dhruv tilted his head to the side. "Why is that so weird a question?"

"Why would she use them?" Jay said. "She has no interest in—well, okay, if Harry showed up, she'd probably ban his ass."

"You know, that I wouldn't mind."

Jay gave him a two-finger salute. "I'll tell her that. But otherwise, there's no reason for her to ban anyone."

"Mmm." Dhruv looked at him. "You really believe in her, and so far, she's only led you in battle."

"It's...that's wrong." Jay shook his head. "You know what you said about Harry? How he always has to win? Gracie isn't in charge of Red Squadron that way. I suppose she does choose where we go and what we do, but it's not absolute. If someone else wanted to do something, they could. It's... She leads by example."

Dhruv settled back in his chair.

"She's not a leader the way Harry would ever think of one," Jay said, at a loss for how else to explain it. "She tells you what she knows, she does what she thinks is right, and she expects other people to do the same. And she collects people who do."

"Interesting." Dhruv frowned. "Still, no one rises without being hated. I know for a fact there are people who don't like her."

"Your Brightstar executives, for one thing," Jay shot back with a tight smile.

Dhruv said nothing in reply, but one eyebrow rose sardonically. "My question is this: if you know her so well and she wants people to do the right thing, where is she going to draw that line, Jay? When someone is interfering, when someone is harassing people? How long until she starts to use those powers Harry gave her? How long until she turns into him just because she can?"

CHAPTER SEVENTEEN

"Ushanas!" Gracie called. "Flank right! *Right!* You have an opening!"

She looked over her shoulder and swore. Ushanas was casting, hands out and ready to call down a storm of fire from the heavens. The Ocru male had robes of a deep red. Theoretically, they should have looked ridiculous on someone so bulky, but they managed to look insanely intimidating instead.

Except Gracie knew that Ushanas was about to get steamrolled by the Piskie rogue that had just come in here.

"Ushanas, get *out* of there!"

"Sec!" Ushanas called back. "One—second—more—and —dammit! Oh, hey." The rogue had gotten him, and in a flurry of strikes, had him down to half-health, but the firestorm had begun, and every enemy in the main battle was now taking damage over time as fireballs thudded to the ground.

Gracie admired the way the game's creators had handled similar animations. If you were on the team targeted, you saw the rain of fire in all its glory. There was roaring, there was burning, your haptics shuddered, and it was hard to see. If you weren't on the team that was targeted, however, you could choose between seeing all of the effects or simply having your opponents glow orange for flame damage, green for earth damage, or blue for frost damage.

Gracie much preferred the immediacy of seeing the fire and reveling in the chaos of the battle—but she had learned at this point that it hampered accuracy too much. She had reluctantly switched to the other effect for now.

They were trying to win, after all, not be distracted by the game's particle effects.

"Come on!" Ushanas called. "Let's go!" He took off, running heavily toward the door at the end of the library.

The rogue, however, was following them. He hopped along behind Ushanas, applying a slowing poison, hamstringing the mage, and avoiding the rain of fire on the other side of the room. Gracie threw her shield at him, but it didn't do quite enough. He stumbled and got a simple stun, which she used to get Ushanas out of the room, but the rogue was back soon after, running down the hallway after them, and disappearing into stealth.

"*Fuck.*" Stealth made him slower, but they had no idea what he was planning right now.

Gracie heaved a sigh as she and Ushanas pelted around the corner and into the long hallway lined with the tumbled-down former suites for Saladin's guests. "If you'd left when I said to, we'd have avoided that kerfuffle."

"Aw, come on." Ushanas didn't seem worried. "I wanted to help our D out a little."

"Let the D handle itself," Gracie said wryly.

"You're *definitely* a chick."

Despite herself, Gracie laughed at that. "Lakhesis, Chowder, what's going on? We don't see you over here."

"You said east, right?"

"I said right," Gracie said. She had her character jump to hurdle a fallen block of stone.

"East is right," Lakhesis said. "On a map."

Gracie groaned. "And on your mini-map?"

"I have mine set to cardinal directions," Lakhesis said.

"And I was following her," Chowder chimed in.

"Oooookay." Gracie wanted to stop and bash her head against one of the stone walls, but she knew that wasn't exactly a productive thing to do at this juncture. "Next time, we...well, let's just use cardinal directions from now on. My bad, I guess."

"We're coming back around," Lakhesis said. "There was nothing over there anyway. And—goddammit!"

"What is it?" Gracie asked, although she had a sinking suspicion she already knew.

"Rogue," Lakhesis said. "Chowder—Chowder, come back. No, stun him. Goddammit."

"He's fast," Chowder said defensively. "And he keeps hopping around like crazy, and I can't...fuck, where the hell *is* he? Come back here, you little devil munchkin thing!"

"Should we go back for them?" Ushanas asked.

Since you're the reason for the rogue being there, yes. Gracie didn't say that. She forced a smile before remembering that Ushanas couldn't see her. "No. Keep running. Guys, corpse-run over to the Dining Hall when you die, okay?"

"It's a little rude to assume we'll die," Lakhesis said, prickly.

"Sorry. If you win—"

"No, we *did* die, I'm just saying."

Gracie wanted to scream with frustration, but she tried to focus on their objective. She came around the corner and skidded to a halt, jerking her torso back in the real world as a reflex for stopping legs that weren't actually moving.

There were five defenders waiting for them. Five? How could there be so many?

She launched into action, throwing her shield and stunning one of them while Ushanas began a group spell, but without any slowing abilities, and without proper melee DPS, they were taken down quickly. Gracie balled her hand into a fist and clenched her teeth as her screen went black and cleared to the blue-and-white of the spirit world.

"They were waiting for us," she said as she waited to resurrect. "Why do you think that was?"

No one answered.

"It was because the rogue warned them," Gracie said, falsely pleasant, "and several of the people there were available because Ushanas had killed them with the firestorm and they resurrected at their own graveyard."

"Whoa, hey." Ushanas sounded annoyed now. "Are you blaming me for this?"

"Yes," Gracie said, her calm breaking now. "Of course, I'm fucking blaming you. I told you to come with me. We had an opening, and you squandered it with defense we didn't need to spend and hamstrung the offense we were trying to run. Yes, I'm blaming you."

"Oh, come on, like you don't think it made sense to help our defense out? There were three people there, and they—"

Gracie wrenched her headset away from her head and stood there staring up at the ceiling of her apartment with her heart pounding.

She was furious. She had spent this entire morning trying to fight through the distraction and constant unpredictability of PvP, and the rest of her team wasn't putting in the effort. They were constantly drawn off-track, helping allies, attacking enemies, and getting pulled into fights that didn't need to concern them.

Yes, PvP was uniquely immersive in *Metamorphosis Online*, but they didn't have the time to waste dicking around right now.

When Harry showed up, they had to be ready. How could Gracie hope to win against him if her team wouldn't even follow her orders?

She felt the haptics shudder and put her headset back on to find that someone had camped her corpse. She stared at the blue-white screen and the countdown timer and wondered if she was actually going out of her mind.

"Gracie?" It was Ushanas. "Are you there?" He sounded genuinely worried, and at that moment, she felt a deep stab of guilt. Her team *was* trying. They were.

It wasn't their fault she was entirely out of her depth here.

"I'm here," she said. "I just needed...a reset. Give me a sec."

"Come on," Ushanas urged.

"I just said—"

"Yeah, and before that, you said for people to run to the other team's graveyard and rez there. Come on." He led the way, his character's robes turned a ghostly white by the world of the dead.

Bemused, Gracie followed him. It was her order, although it had been back from when they had thought they might still win.

As if Ushanas could sense her thoughts, he turned to look at her over his shoulder. "You didn't give up, did you? Because if so, I'm afraid I'll have to believe you got replaced by your evil twin. Does your sister look a lot like you or something?"

"My sister wouldn't get near a video game if you threatened her life," Gracie replied, rolling her eyes. "She's off on Nantucket or something, wearing seersucker and planning her surprised face for when her boyfriend proposes on the 4th of July."

"I mean, that *does* sound like an evil twin, so…"

Gracie laughed. They were close to the other team's graveyard, and they saw Lakhesis and Chowder waiting there, still in the spirit world. The other two waved, and Lakhesis motioned for them to circle up. All of them leaned in, Lakhesis standing on her tiptoes. The human was surrounded by two Ocru and an Aosi, so she was the shortest by far.

"All right, gang," Lakhesis started. "They think they have this thing in the bag, but what have we learned from Gracie over the past few weeks?"

"Trust her instincts," Chowder said.

"Listen to her orders," Ushanas added.

"Guys, I am right here; this is a bit weird."

"Above all," Lakhesis continued, ignoring Gracie's interjection, "no matter how long the shot is, never. Give. Up!"

"Never give up!" Ushanas and Chowder chorused. They looked at Gracie.

"Come on," Ushanas said again. He was laughing. "Maybe you suck at PvP right now, but we started out Team Underdog, and that's our jam."

Gracie's jaw dropped. She knew what he was doing, and she was trying not to laugh. "I do *not* suck at PvP."

"Oh, really?" Ushanas did the side-to-side head bob for a sassy comeback. "Then *prove it.*"

"Game on." Gracie looked around. "We ready?"

"Ready!" the other three yelled.

They rezzed just in time to see the other team's flag carrier sprinting dead out through the oasis. She had broken away from her pursuers, and she and her attendant healer seemed to think they were in the clear.

They were very, very wrong. Gracie charged out of cover and took the healer out sideways with a shield bash. Chowder went to town on the flag carrier in a blur of short swords, and Ushanas was handing out DoTs like they were candy. Lakhesis, meanwhile, helped Chowder burn the flag carrier down while saving her interrupt until Gracie yelled,"NOW!"

Lakhesis stunned the healer, who was a half-second away from pulling out the lifesaving heal, and the flag carrier went down in a heap.

"Go, go, go!" Gracie yelled.

The team charged into the enemy headquarters, Ushanas throwing one last fireball at the healer and chortling. "He ate that one in the face. Pro tip, kids: don't eat fireballs."

"Citation needed," Gracie told him. She ran for the flag. "Lakhesis, me or you?"

"You," Lakhesis said without hesitation. "You have more HP, and I like DPS more." She peeled away and began running for the exit. "East or west?"

"West, and right-o." Gracie grabbed the flag and headed for the west corridor with Ushanas and Chowder in tow. "All right, we're about to have everyone on our ass, and we didn't manage to bring a healer, so just keep an eye on your health bar, okay, kids?"

"I thought Caspian was unemployed right now," Ushanas grumbled. "What use is an unemployed healer if they can't save us from the consequences of our own decisions?"

"Good point," Chowder rumbled.

Gracie let the conversation wash over her. She was smiling, although she didn't chime in. She had scanned to her left as they dashed out of the building and seen the bulk of the other team heading right for them.

"Get ready, guys. Ushanas, find a hiding spot."

"Way ahead of you." Ushanas waved from halfway up a ruined stairwell as Gracie and Chowder sprinted by. "Squishies always have a good hiding spot planned."

"Excellent." Gracie, much to her own sorrow, was not able to turn around and watch when she heard the fire start raining down. From Ushanas' hysterical laughter, however, she assumed that the other team had not expected to come around the corner and be trapped in a fireball-filled hellscape without any easy escape.

"Three got through," Ushanas reported. "A rogue, a sender, and a warrior."

"Chowder, Lakhesis." Gracie didn't look.

"On it." Chowder stopped and pivoted in one smooth motion. "Hello, sender. Nice low health bar you got there. Would be a shame if something were to happen to it."

"Threw another DoT on that rogue," Ushanas called. "Now he won't be able to go into stealth."

"You're a dream," Gracie called back. She saw Lakhesis hurtle past her in the opposite direction to join the melee, and the two tanks waved cheerily at each other.

Gracie switched to the main team chat. "I don't suppose there's a healer anywhere near me. I'm coming out of the west hallway and getting close to our headquarters."

"Hide for a second," a new voice said, and Gracie shrank into the shadows.

Another flag carrier ran out of their headquarters and toward the enemy base. Gracie waited until they were past, then snuck into the library and went to a dead sprint to get to their empty flag stand.

VICTORY, the screen announced in huge letters, and there was a cheer from her teammates.

"Look at that," Ushanas said privately. "You were right."

"Sorry I was an ass," Gracie said. She heaved a sigh.

"You don't have much patience for losing, do you?" Ushanas was clearly smiling. "It's been a strength before. You can make it one again if you choose."

CHAPTER EIGHTEEN

Alex was out with Sydney for dinner, so Gracie wolfed down a tuna sandwich and a beer and logged back into the game. By the time she arrived, Caspian was there, chatting seriously with Chowder, Kevin, Lakhesis, and Freon.

"Ushanas says she'll be back soon," Lakhesis told them.

"Ushanas is a she?" Chowder asked in surprise.

"Pretty sure," Lakhesis said.

"Huh." Chowder seemed very preoccupied with the idea.

"And Alan will be here soon as well," Kevin said. "He came over to my place for dinner to meet Jamie, here, and he's driving home to log on now. I have to say, it just feels *weird* not to call you Caspian."

Caspian laughed. "You *could* call me Caspian. I don't mind, you know. I haven't been offended when you slipped up, just like you weren't offended when I totally botched the pancakes."

"You botched *pancakes*?" Chowder asked skeptically.

"Even I can make pancakes."

"I got cocky," Caspian said. "I've never been able to make them properly, but I was on a roll, and…they just turned out horribly."

"Which is why we have McDonald's," Kevin said. "Although, I'm beginning to remember why I stopped eating that stuff. I'm not twenty anymore, and my stomach isn't made of iron."

"Where are you all?" Gracie asked curiously. She had walked into their usual tavern, only to find it empty.

"Oh, sorry." Kevin sent her a party invite. "We're up at the temple. You know, where things first went south?"

"Yeah?"

"Yeah. Come join us." He didn't give any other details.

Gracie frowned curiously as she headed their way. They were bantering back and forth, throwing around lazy insults about each other's play style, into which were mixed some genuinely good pieces of advice. That seemed to be how they'd taken to helping each other out these days, and she didn't mind as long as the information got across and everyone was in on the joke.

She started up the hill during a particularly spirited round of "yo mama" jokes, including jokes about intellect buffs, equipment slots, and whether or not Chowder's mother was large enough that they needed an AoE spell to do damage to her. Gracie snorted at that last joke. She was high enough level now that she didn't need to pay attention to the patrolling ghosts in this zone. Instead, they were trying very hard not to notice her.

Gracie could still remember their initial climb up this hill. It was one of the first times they'd had Ushanas on board, and they'd been carefully planning out their strategy.

For a different boss than the one they got.

Instead of the ice boss, they had wound up with the first boss in Harry's quest line, and Gracie smiled to remember the way they had thrown desperate suggestions at one another and banded together to defeat it. It was something she had loved about those bosses, despite the stress of them: you never knew what was coming. You had to think on your feet and go by instinct.

Like PvP.

She slowed to a stop at the entrance to the temple, her mind whirling.

It was true. She loved pitting her wits against game bosses who forced her to think outside the box and react cleverly. And what boss required more outside-the-box thinking than a human opponent, someone who adapted to your play style and acted illogically sometimes? She had a very low tolerance for failure, and she'd allowed those experiences to scare her away instead of forcing her to adapt...which was the best-case scenario for Harry.

She was damned if she was going to let him win because she couldn't learn something new.

"Gracie?" She whirled with a muffled exclamation and saw Jay standing there. He waved, then blew a kiss.

She sighed. "You know, I wish we could actually kiss. That would be much nicer."

"Guys?" Kevin said. "Public channel."

"*OH SHIT!*" Gracie clapped her hands over her mouth. "Don't mind me. I'm just going to go sink through the floor. It's fine. Everything's fine."

"Oh, don't do that." Caspian was laughing. "You two are cute."

"They're together?" Chowder asked. "Did everyone else know that? How do I not know *anything* about this guild?"

"They've kept it on the DL," Lakhesis said. "But they're super adorably awkward around each other."

Gracie sank her face into her hands.

"Ignore them," Jay said on a private channel. He held out his hand, and she put hers near it. There was a pause while they stared at each other's hands, and then, in unison, both of them made a fist and did an airy fist-bump. Jay emoted a laugh. "Who says romance is dead?"

"Not me." Gracie grinned at him. "A ruined temple filled with ghosts and zombies? You really know how to treat a girl."

"I don't want to brag," Jay said, "but it looks like there's a considerable amount of mold as well."

Gracie laughed. They were strolling toward the main group, and they came around the corner to find that the team had laid out a feast by the view out over Kithara. Gracie looked at it all in interest as she walked over.

"Holy crap, that's a lot of food."

"Remember how Alan and I were learning to cook?" Caspian asked. He swept his hands over the array of dishes. "Well, here you go!"

"If you knew how good his cooking was in real life, you'd be as hungry as I am right now," Kevin commented. "I bet you could make a roast pig."

"In your apartment?" Caspian asked skeptically.

"I have a balcony."

Gracie laughed. "So, a pixelated picnic. I love you guys."

"And we love you," Kevin said, giving her an elaborate bow. "And we figured, what better place to hang out and strategize? We've heard you had a few successes in Saladin's Keep today."

"We did indeed." Gracie settled her character down on a chunk of stone. "It's not my forte, I'll tell you that, but Ushanas whipped my butt into shape, and I'm definitely not about to let Harry win this confrontation."

"Speaking of which," Jay said bluntly, "I've been tasked by Dan and Dhruv with finding out what he's planning, so if any of you have any ideas, let me know. I don't know that I'll pass *everything* on to them, of course, but it'll be nice to know what we're going to be facing."

Gracie smiled at him. "They might have really changed their tune," she pointed out.

"They might." He sounded troubled. "I don't think they trust you as a queen."

"Well, to be fair to them, I haven't had any official training." She noticed his hesitation before he laughed and reminded herself to ask him about it later. "In the meantime, unless anyone else has a different gut feeling, I'm definitely going to be preparing for us to face Harry in a PvP match of some sort, and—what was that?"

"What was what?" Jay looked over his shoulder. Gracie slid off the stone and headed for the edge of the temple, her heart pounding all of a sudden. They had teammates coming to join them here, but the person she'd seen was trying to hide, not join them. Which meant—

She came around a tumbled-down wall and gave a grim nod. "Yaro. What a surprise."

CHAPTER NINETEEN

Yaro smiled at Gracie, a sharp-toothed smile on the pale, sickly-looking face. He was still dressed in the Level 1 robes, so she couldn't imagine how he'd made it up here without being killed by a bunch of ghosts, but she wasn't going to waste time on logistics right now.

"What the hell are you doing here?" Gracie asked him bluntly.

"I came to see you," Yaro said, his tone dripping with insincere warmth. "I wanted to watch the queen hold court."

"Would you *stop* it with the queen bullshit?" Gracie's temper was spiking. Everything was coming home to her now: the PvP, the constant uncertainty of what was coming next, the fact that people were trying to sabotage her, and they didn't have the first idea of who she was or what she was even trying to do.

The fact that she didn't really have the first idea of what she was even trying to do.

Fuck my life.

Yaro smiled again. "You don't like being called a queen? I thought you earned the title. That's what you told me last time, isn't it?"

Gracie's hands clenched, and when Yaro laughed, she remembered too late that he could see her gestures.

"Why did you come?" she asked again. "Because it wasn't to observe me with my friends, that's for damned sure."

"You're wrong," Yaro said simply. "You don't know the first thing about me."

"And you don't know the first thing about me!" Gracie shot back. "You're acting like you know some deep, dark secret of mine, but you don't. I didn't cheat my way to this. I didn't take anything from you—unless you're Harry, of course, in which case, you deserved it."

"You see, you're inconsistent," Yaro said. "You did take something. That is where it begins and ends. You took something that was not yours, and you've used it to rise above those who should be your equals."

Gracie had nothing to say. There was nothing to say to that.

Yaro was right, after all. It was no use saying she hadn't stolen anything or cheated. She might have fallen ass-backward into the quest, but she had known how to give it back—and she hadn't done so. She had known that the quest wasn't something Dan and Dhruv intended, and while the two of them could easily claim that their vision of the game was just as important as Harry's...

She definitely couldn't.

"You thought you deserved this?" Yaro asked. "Or did you just want to be the queen and have a pretty crown and listen to your teammates fawning over you and telling you how smart and wonderful you were? Did you actually want loyalty or just sycophants?"

"That's enough." Jay's voice was hard. He had come to stand by Gracie's shoulder. "I don't know who the hell you are, but you need to stop stalking her. This isn't anything to do with you."

"It's not anything to do with you either," Yaro said. He crossed his arms over his chest and tilted his head slightly. "You just wanted to be close to power, didn't you?"

Jay started to respond, but Gracie cut him off with a swipe of her hand. Caspian and Kevin were at her other shoulder, and she felt more embarrassed than anything to have her team standing up for her. After all, wasn't Yaro right? Didn't Gracie like being in charge? Didn't she like winning?

"No answer to that?" Yaro asked. "Typical. You thought you could come in here and all the men would fall all over themselves to—"

"*Shut up.*" Gracie's temper blazed to life. "Shut. Up."

Yaro fell silent, but Gracie could sense his smirk through the internet.

"You want to know why I held off coming here for so long?" Gracie snapped at him. "Because every other group I played with treated me like shit for being a woman. They expected me to be available to them; they told me how they wanted me to dress, how they wanted me to do my hair and my makeup like I fucking owed it to them to be their personal idea of a fuckable gamer girl."

No one said anything. Yaro's posture had changed slightly, although Gracie didn't know what to make of that, and her team had stepped back.

"You know why I love these people?" Gracie demanded, sweeping her hands out to indicate the guild. "It's because when they found out I was a chick, they didn't give a damn. They didn't take me any less seriously, and they didn't stop thinking I was a good tank. They didn't treat every interaction like it was some sort of power struggle someone had to win. They suggested things to me and took my suggestions." She was heaving for breath. She wanted to scream and scream and never stop. "I walked into this world, and it was the most beautiful thing I'd ever seen, and you know what? You were right the other day, okay? You were right about my family. They do think I'm a piece of shit. I'm a disappointment, okay? I had a shit job. I didn't have a boyfriend. I never got my Ph.D. And here, in this insane world with magic and faeries and swords the size of my whole body…" she was shaking, tears leaking out the bottom of her headset, "this was the one place I felt like I could make a difference."

Yaro said nothing to that.

"She did make a difference," Caspian said. "I found friends in her guild. They helped me become a better healer without worrying about their own ranks."

"I was going through a really bad time," Lakhesis said. "My sister died, and my parents…haven't coped well. They didn't want to see me anymore since it just reminded them about Kara being gone. I came here because I needed a place to get away. I don't know what I would have done without this world, and I don't know what I would have done without these people telling me jokes and just giving me an escape."

Gracie looked at her, her heart twisting. She had never

guessed that behind Lakhesis' bright, cheery persona was something like this, but now that the other woman mentioned it, she could remember the slightly brittle edge to her voice sometimes, and the way she was just a bit *too* cheerful.

"I hadn't been worried about whether I stood up and did the right thing," Jay said. "It hadn't even been on my radar. Gracie showed me what it looked like to care, even when the people you cared about weren't part of the real world."

Yaro had paused, but now he stirred to life again. "Very touching stories," he said, and his voice was far too sweet, "but none of it changes the fact that you cheated your way here. You didn't play as hard as others did to win your ranking. You found your title by accident. How are we supposed to trust that you should have this power?"

Gracie looked down at the ground, her vision blurring. None of this mattered to Yaro. Why should it? He hated her, and no matter that she refuted each point he threw at her, the goalposts would only keep moving.

She'd learned long ago that those fights were unwinnable. Her parents hadn't ever let her accomplishments get in the way of favoring her sister, the guys at her college were sure as hell not going to believe she was there on merit, and the men she played D&D with weren't willing to see her as a person instead of a bundle of physical features.

There would be no winning this. To her surprise, her anger began to drain away. She should hate this man, she thought. Part of her was still raging at the absolute unfairness of it all. He was being an asshole, and she shouldn't have to deal with that.

But she would. It was just part of life. She was angry because of everything she had been through, and the same must be true of him. And maybe, just maybe, Dhruv had been right—that this world could be the place they worked all that out so they didn't hurt their friends and family outside *Metamorphosis*.

"You shouldn't trust me," Gracie told Yaro. "You shouldn't trust anyone with power. Anyone who can control people is untrustworthy."

Her entire team was silent. Alan and Ushanas, who had just arrived up the road from Kithara, had stopped a few yards away, unsure what was going on.

Yaro said nothing.

"Who you should trust is these people," Gracie said, jerking her head at the ones around her. "Because they're the ones who call me on my shit. *That's* what you should trust; that's the team I've surrounded myself with."

There was a long pause.

"And when they disagree, and you get rid of them?" Yaro asked. "What then? You'll be a dictator with no one to stop you."

Gracie shrugged helplessly. "It's a chance I'm willing to take because I think I'd rather lose all of this than lose these friends. And if everything goes wrong, if it all goes to hell...well, at least I'll know I tried."

"Tried what?" Yaro pressed. "Why do you even need this?"

"Because there's an asshole who wants to be the thought police, and another asshole who hates him and keeps taking money over being ethical," Gracie said, "and both of them are fucking around in the servers. I'd like to be able to do my damned job as a tank and keep that aggro off all the rest of you."

"Nice spin to put on it," Yaro said, "when really, you're just a power-hungry bitch who wants all the men to be drooling over her."

Gracie laughed. She couldn't help herself. "You really think you can find an insult I haven't heard before?" she asked him. "You believe you can come up with something that'll devastate me? Look, I don't know why you hate me. You won't say. But if you need to hate me, fine. I'll still be your tank."

She turned to walk away, and she heard Yaro's voice again—but he wasn't speaking to her, he was speaking to Jay.

"I guess she *is* the woman you thought."

"*Dhruv?*" Jay sounded halfway between shocked and furious. "What the hell?"

"You think I'm going to be the worst she encounters?" Dhruv asked. "She was tempted to ban me at the start. She tried to explain herself to me, and she won't be able to explain herself to everyone. But in the end, she's focusing on what matters."

Gracie turned back, shaking her head. "You could have just asked."

"No," Dhruv said. He shrugged. "I *couldn't* just ask this. Power changes people, and this power was what Harry created for himself."

"I know that," Gracie said. "I knew that the first day you got on my case and I wanted to ban you. This is how Harry saw people: ants in an ant farm, rats in a maze. He wanted to pick and choose people until he ended up with some fucked-up utopia where all the people thought exactly what he did and did exactly what he wanted and never called him on his bullshit. That's where his powers lead; I know that."

Dhruv said nothing.

Gracie walked closer. "That's why I'm saving them for him."

"He'll find a way to take them away from you," Dhruv warned her.

"Maybe. But I've beaten him before, and I'll do it again. I'm not going to turn into a power-hungry maniac in the meantime." She shrugged. "Happy?"

"Eh." Dhruv shrugged back.

Gracie rolled her eyes. "Do you want some food?" she asked with excessive politeness.

Dhruv gave a sound that might have been a laugh. "No, you have a good feast. It was nice to meet you as a queen." He disappeared without any more fanfare, logging out with a little *bloop*.

"Argh." Jay rubbed his forehead. "I hate that man."

"I see why he did it," Gracie said. "Better it was him who tested me than some random jackass."

"Oh, he did mention," Jay said, "that he wouldn't mind if you banned Harry."

"Good," Gracie replied. "Because I plan to."

CHAPTER TWENTY

"Anyone want to tell me where we're going?" Grok asked on the main channel.

Harkness shushed him, but not before Thad looked over his shoulder at the Ocru. In reality, Grok was about 5'4" and incredibly thin, the sort of person who could gobble down a whole pizza and ask for more an hour later. He tended to hunch his shoulders and make himself look even shorter, and he was doing that now as their transport zoomed across the desert. He turned away first, and Thad looked back to the desert ahead of them.

No one else said anything on the main channel, and he had the suspicion that they were talking behind his back.

They didn't like Yesuan. The new Piskie healer was the subject of considerable speculation. They'd noticed that he was on one of the team accounts, and they'd also noticed that Thad seemed to take his orders.

And he gave a *lot* of orders. Yesuan didn't seem to give a damn if people liked him. Sometimes, Thad even thought

Yesuan *wanted* people to hate him. He was certainly behaving the right way if that was what he wanted.

Right now, for instance, Yesuan was the one steering the transport. He'd come into the guild's morning practice, announced that they were going somewhere, and left without waiting to see if anyone would follow him. He'd led the way to the far end of the transport docks and taken one of the ones that was already there. As far as Thad had known, those were just ornamental, but Yesuan seemed to be able to drive them.

If Jamie were still here, he'd be asking worried-sounding questions about all of this.

Thad crossed his arms over his chest and tried not to growl his annoyance with his former healer. He'd built Jamie up to what he was. Sure, Jamie had shown natural talent, but it was Thad's investment of resources and gear that had allowed Jamie to level so quickly, and it was Thad's offer of a job that had gotten Jamie into the guild when Thad was first approached by Brightstar. Thad had taken the time to court healers and the very best DPS there was. He gave them his time. He gave them leeway. He gave them perks.

And this was how Jamie had repaid him.

Yesuan looked at him now. "They don't like you," the Piskie said.

Thad stiffened but did not look over. He checked that he was on a private channel before responding, "Do you have a point?"

"They *shouldn't* like you," Yesuan said. "You forget that. You want to be their leader and have them be your friends."

"No, I don't." Wanting to win a popularity contest was

like grade school all over again, and he was definitely past that.

The transport shuddered to a halt, and the Piskie looked at Thad coldly. "I have no patience for lies and self-deception," Yesuan said. "And I don't have time for fools who can't understand basic logic, either. Stop acting like a child, or I will leave you all here and find another guild to serve my purpose."

Thad looked at him furiously. The rest of the guild, noticing that the transport had stopped, was coming over, and Thad gestured for them to stay away.

"Are you sure about that?" Thad asked venomously. "You wanted good players who knew how to follow orders, and you've got them. Who else are you going to get to do this without asking questions you don't want to answer?"

For a moment, he thought Yesuan would call his bluff, but then the Piskie nodded. "Interesting," Yesuan said. "So you do have a backbone after all. But you're still lying to yourself."

Thad rolled his eyes and sighed. "Can we not do this? I don't want to have a philosophical discussion right now."

"Of course not," Yesuan said. "And it doesn't matter anyway."

With that, he started driving again, and Thad frowned at him. What did that mean?

It meant that Yesuan was insufferably pretentious, that was what it meant. Thad had seen enough by this point to know that. He rolled his eyes and went back to watching the desert. There was nothing out here, no plants or scrub brush, and the dunes and sandstone bluffs were steep enough that people would not have been able to get here by foot or mount. Then Harkness shouted and pointed, and the whole group hurried over to one side of the transport to get a look.

Thad frowned. Yesuan was guiding them in a lazy circle around a full replica of Saladin's Keep. Or *was* this Saladin's Keep?

"It's a real place in the game," Yesuan said, sensing Thad's stare. "The instance is different, of course, but the place exists."

"Son of a bitch." Thad had not spent much time doing PvP, but he had to admit that he'd enjoyed Saladin's Keep. There was something appealing about running around abandoned buildings, especially the ruins of former splendor.

With the verdant oasis in the center of the keep, the place had an amazing feel to it, clearly a desert without feeling too bright or too dry. The game's developers had really gone all out in the keep, too. Sometimes gold coins or jewels winked in the sunlight, and people claimed they saw ghosts and heard courtly music on nighttime runs.

He turned to Yesuan as the Piskie deposited them near one of the gates. "What are we doing here?"

"Getting ready," Yesuan said simply. "I gave you the instructions. You'll run skirmishes against each other while I watch—and explore the ruins. There are things here I need to find."

He hopped off the platform and disappeared into the ruins, and Thad stared after him with a frown.

He did not like this dude, whoever he was—but he'd be lying if he said that the man's absolute, uncaring arrogance wasn't at least a little bit interesting. After all, Thad had been lying when he said he didn't care if his guildmates liked him. Of course, he cared. Who wouldn't?

Yesuan, apparently.

Thad turned to his team. All of them were here, not just the first-string players he brought into the dungeons with him. Yesuan had insisted that everyone come to these practice sessions. That meant Thad was looking at twenty-eight players since Brightstar refused to sponsor a full-sized guild of fifty.

"We'll be running skirmishes," Thad said. "Even numbers on the roster will start in the dining hall, odd numbers will start in the library. Yesuan's not on anyone's team. Harkness, you do invites for the even team. I'll take the odd team."

They partied up, and Thad nodded at all of them. The teams were a little unbalanced, but it would be an interesting exercise that way. "We focus on AoE and snares," he told them. "I don't want either flag carrier to go a single second without being under some negative effect. That means I expect you to arrange your defense and protect your flag carrier. Yesuan will be observing."

"Why—" Grok began.

"The skirmish begins in two minutes," Thad said. "Teams, get to your bases."

He didn't want people asking questions, particularly ones he couldn't answer.

Thad led the way to the library. Their team had none of the healers, which annoyed him—but it made the other team comparably less deadly. He'd take it. He checked his team as he ran. They had Preacher, the guild's highest-ranked rogue, and Kala, a summoner who specialized in demons. She already had her amarok out, the ice-wolf's white fur glinting blue in the sunlight.

Demon Syndicate's off-tank, AreTee, was on the other team, as were two of the mages, Harkness and Anubis. Thad had DreadPRoberts, nicknamed Deep, and Blast, and FaceMelt, known as Face.

They could make this work.

"I want Preacher and Deep on defense," he said. "I'll run offense with Kala, Face, and Blast. Kala, feel free to peel off if someone needs snaring."

"Roger," Kala said. Like most female characters in the game, Kala was played by a man. She had dark brown skin and spiky bright-blue hair that Thad was beginning to think should be changed. PvE bosses didn't care what players looked like, but a noteworthy target was easier to select in a PvP game.

He'd mention that to Jack, her player, later.

"Everyone else," Thad directed, "make yourself useful. After this game, we'll give specific feedback."

The timer Thad had set dinged, and he ran out of the library toward the oasis, not waiting for any of the rest of the team to weigh in. He had the vague sense that some of them were spreading out across the keep, and he shook his head, annoyed. The keep's setup was a trap, with the long, open corridors not easy to get in and out of, and considerable time lost with running the long way around.

He'd be giving them a talking to about that.

Or Yesuan would. A tight knot of anxiety formed in Thad's chest. He didn't like the idea of Yesuan giving feedback while the rest of the team stared at Thad and wondered why he wasn't in charge anymore.

But he'd been looking, and there were no other healers to be found. If he didn't want to use Yesuan, he was fucked. And if he did, he had to put up with this.

As he ran past the oasis, he saw a flash of pink hair. Yesuan was lurking amongst the trees, presumably to watch all of them without being seen. Thad swore silently. He didn't like being watched by someone who seemed determined to find fault. When he stole another glance, however, he saw that Yesuan didn't even seem to be watching anyone. Instead, he was pacing between bushes and plants, peering intently at the ground.

What was he looking for?

Thad didn't care. He wanted all of this to be over, and there was only one way to do that: get ready for the next month-first and pay whatever price Yesuan was asking. He had also been reaching out to other prospective funders, wondering if they might pay for him to run one of the other sponsored guilds. It was possible. He had options, he told himself.

He had options.

For now, he would just get through this. Whatever Yesuan wanted, Thad didn't care. If it meant getting back at Callista and Jamie, he'd do it.

CHAPTER TWENTY-ONE

When Jay arrived at work the next morning, he was not surprised to see a summons to one of the conference rooms. When he got there, Dan, Dhruv, and Sam were sitting next to a somewhat smaller spread of donuts and coffee.

Jay was going to need to spend whole nights running dungeons at this rate.

"That was a dirty trick," he said to Dhruv as he picked out a donut.

"We thought you liked donuts," Sam said, sounding confused.

"Not the donuts," Jay said. He got himself a cup of coffee and shot a glance at Dhruv. "You going to explain or should I?"

"I want to see how you sum it up," Dhruv said, after a moment's consideration.

Jay reflected that he really should have known better than to expect Dhruv to have any shame about his actions. The man was immune to normal forms of social pressure.

He sat down and gazed at Dan and Sam, both of whom looked intrigued.

"Dhruv wanted to know whether Gracie was going to turn into a tyrant," Jay began, then took a bite of donut. "So, naturally, the way he decided to do that was to see how hard he could poke the bear before he got banned."

Dan gave a deep sigh and looked at Dhruv.

"I used what I knew of her to see if I could get under her skin," Dhruv said, entirely unconcerned. "And I *did* get under her skin, and I do still have some concerns—but not big ones. She's able to hold her temper. She hasn't caved to the temptation of muting people or banning them. We're lucky, as far as things go, that she's the one who found the quest."

"What did you do?" Dan demanded, not at all distracted by Dhruv's explanation. "Seriously, what did you *do*?"

"He made an alt and followed Gracie around, insulting her," Jay explained.

"I also sent her emails," Dhruv admitted.

"You *what*?" Jay demanded at the same time Dan said, "You realize that's actually a legal liability—"

"Okay." Sam tapped the flat of his hand on the table. Everyone looked at him in surprise, and he gave a tight smile. "Long story short, Dhruv's concerns are put to rest and Jay's not incandescently angry, so I assume everything resolved itself, and we actually do have work to do today. We need to focus on that."

Everyone nodded, chastened. Sam rarely asserted his authority, but when he did, you tended to go along with it —even if you were technically his boss.

"We're looking at anything vaguely related to PvP," Sam

told Jay. "We know that last time, Harry hijacked dungeons and inserted himself as the boss. What we don't know is how he intends to confront Gracie this time, beyond everyone's general suspicion that it will happen on one of the battlegrounds."

Jay nodded. "There are a few main possibilities, right?" His mind was running ahead, and he let the words out with no filter, hoping he wouldn't say anything ridiculous. "So, it's possible he's doing the same thing he did with the quest: eventually, she'll go into the right battleground, and he'll be there waiting. But that's tricky."

"Especially because he shouldn't be able to make a character," Dan said. "We blocked him from doing that, and to my knowledge, he hasn't gotten around it."

"That's one hell of a block," Jay exclaimed.

"Didn't you wonder why he hadn't shown up to claim that quest?" Dhruv asked. "It's why he went into the game as the bosses. He could still do that; he just couldn't be there as a player. As far as we know, he still can't, but none of the battlegrounds have NPCs in them that he could inhabit."

"Quarry Ridge has the potions master," Sam said, surprising Jay with his knowledge. He took their surprised looks in stride with a small smile. "Once we started focusing on PvP, I thought it would be prudent to do my research."

"Okay, so Quarry Ridge has the potions master," Dan said. "Do we focus there, then?"

There was a pause while they all thought.

"No," Jay said. "We focus on how he's going to force the confrontation. That's more important. It'll be something like a duel mechanic, right? Something she can't ignore."

The other three nodded. Dan was taking notes in scrawling longhand that looked like it was filled with symbols.

"And is it going to be one on one?" Jay asked. "Or as teams? I'm guessing one on one because he was so crazy about that last time—"

"Crazy?" Dhruv raised an eyebrow. "Because I would have guessed teams, but I wasn't able to hear anything he said in the last dungeon last time, only Gracie's responses." He looked at this watch but made no comment on why.

"He basically challenged her to a one-on-one fight," Jay explained. "He was a boss, so that would be stupid as hell to do, but he kept calling her a coward. Much like you did," he added whimsically.

"Yeah, yeah," Dhruv said. "Die mad about it." He gave Jay a grin that conveyed the friendliest "Fuck you" Jay had ever seen.

Out of the corner of his eye, Jay saw Dan and Sam exchange looks. Sam shrugged slightly, and Dan shook his head with a sigh.

"Anyway," Dhruv said, "Harry was never good at PvP, so my guess is that he'll have a team. Whether or not he'll let *her* have one."

"That, I think, depends on when whatever mechanic it is was built," Dan interjected. "As Jay pointed out yesterday —Dhruv told me about your list, Jay—he didn't write the quest until we started trying to boot him. Was this written at the same time, or is he utilizing some other mechanic we don't know about? Something he put in there before? The earlier it was put in, the fairer I think we can assume it is." He gave Jay and Sam a tight smile. "Harry loves to think of himself as fair," he explained. "And then someone wins, and he makes things less fair. So, you can tell how fair an encounter with him will be depending on whether or not you're at the first stage of the conflict."

Despite himself, Jay laughed. He could just imagine that: Harry, determined that he knew best, wanting to rule by right of strength—and then later wanting to rule by right of winning, no matter how much he had to slant the encounter in his favor to win it.

"Okay," he said a moment later. "So, here's my guess: whatever he's going to do, it's something that was already in the game. He envisioned a world with kings and war. You two have been pretty cagey about it, but it seems like there's the possibility for factions to form and war to break out. That's basically a forced PvP encounter, right? So, I'd bet there's something already in there." Then a thought coalesced: "*Demon Syndicate.*"

"Huh?" Dhruv asked. He exchanged looks with Dan.

Dan settled his face into a blank customer service smile. "I don't think it would necessarily be wise to reach out to Demon Syndicate," he said blandly. "Certain...situations have—"

"No, not us reaching out," Jay said. "Harry." Everyone stared at him blankly, and Jay wanted to beat his head on the table. "Harry needs a team, right? That's where we're going. So he needs a bunch of people who are willing to side with him against the game's creators and some goddess-queen hybrid thing. They have to be good, and they have to have some animosity he can use. He's all about that, isn't he? About getting into people's heads and making them want to do things for him?"

Dan's mouth opened and closed twice. "Oh, dear God."

Dhruv didn't waste time processing the idea emotionally. He looked at Sam. "Do we still have the link into Demon Syndicate's feed?" he asked.

"Yes, but that was just to the account they were using for watching Red Squadron," Sam said. "I don't actually know how they set it up."

"We can make another one," Dhruv said, "it would just be quicker to go through a channel that was already built. We'll want to look at what they're doing now."

"I can check." Dan stirred to life and opened his laptop. "Give me a character name. No, never mind, I'll go through the guild lookup." He tapped his fingers on the trackpad as he waited for things to load, then began searching. He murmured to himself as he did so, checking and cross-referencing, and after a few searches, he started to frown.

The frown got deeper as he continued.

"Is something wrong?" Jay asked.

"Kind of." Dan sat back. "They're in a non-active zone. Well, a part of the Sea of Sand they shouldn't be able to get to, and they're all there."

"What part?" Dhruv stood up and went to look, along with Sam and Jay. They peered over Dan's shoulder, and all of them frowned when they saw the zone name.

Saladin's Keep

"You know that zone is active, right?" Jay asked quizzically.

"This isn't the battleground," Dan said. He pointed. "There'd be a battleground notation in front of it if it were

—and there would be no major zone. *This* is the actual place. It's in the Sea of Sand, and we were theoretically going to open it up at some point. That's how you all had that Christmas party PvP there," he added to Jay.

"Oh," Jay said. "So, they're not supposed to be able to get there?"

"No," Dhruv said flatly. "They're not. The only way is by flying transport, which you'd have to be able to utilize. Someone helped them."

"I think we have our answer," Sam said a moment later. He'd been scanning the list of names and typed something into his phone. "They lost a healer, right? Well, now they have a recruit called TrialHealer whose account is five days old, and who is nonetheless top-level and has a full set of Elite armor."

He held up his phone, which displayed the global rankings lookup, and there was a long pause while they all stared.

"I didn't think he'd ever in a million years go for a Piskie character," Dhruv remarked finally.

"How. The hell. Did he get into the game?" Dan asked far too pleasantly.

"Account lookup," Sam suggested. They all leaned over the screen again as Dan searched until he gave them all a look. Then they stood up while he kept typing.

"Registered to..." Dan frowned, "an LLC, which means we had to have given them a dispensation, and—"

"Front Range," Sam said. "That's Brightstar. They funnel their charity and sponsorships and so on through there."

Dan went very still. "So they're now employing Harry?"

he said. This time the pleasantness was so strong that Jay found himself breaking out in a cold sweat.

"Apparently," he said. He chewed his lip. "If they made him his own account, they must be, right?"

"Possibly," Sam said. He sounded cautious.

Dan rounded on him. "*Possibly*? He's using their account. What other explanation—"

"We don't *know*," Sam said patiently. "We should find out before doing anything rash, that's all I'm saying. For one thing, we have an active contract with them, so knowing exactly how they breached it would be useful."

"How who breached what contract?" asked a new voice.

Jay looked up, and his jaw dropped. "Gracie?"

There she was, standing with her hands in the pockets of some rolled-up jeans, an oversized green sweatshirt draped over her slim frame, and her long light-brown hair pulled into a ponytail.

"We flew her in," Dhruv said. Jay now remembered him looking at his phone and his watch. "We figured it was past time to join forces officially."

CHAPTER TWENTY-TWO

"Gracie." Jay looked like he'd been hit by a truck.

It was him, but he was real. For the first time, Gracie could reach out and touch him if she wanted, and her fingers wouldn't go right through him. She was shaking, she realized—adrenaline pounding through her veins. She'd been on the lookout as the receptionist led her through the halls, but it had still been a shock to come around the corner and see Jay.

"Hi," she managed.

One of the other three, a man who looked to be about forty with thinning hair, cleared his throat. "We'll give you two a moment."

"We have things to do," said a man Gracie assumed was Dhruv.

The first man interrupted him. "A moment," he reiterated. He ushered the other two men out firmly, giving Gracie a nod as he went by. Then the door shut and they were alone in the room.

Neither she nor Jay moved for a good few seconds,

and when they did, it was to edge closer to each other very slowly. Gracie reached out, and Jay did the same. They were both, she realized, having trouble believing the other person was actually there. Then, at the same time, they curled their hands into fists and did a fist bump.

That broke the weird unreality of the moment, and they both dissolved into laughter. Gracie leaned on the table with one hand, hand over her stomach. The problem was, she didn't seem to be able to stop laughing. Her head was a whirl of thoughts, from everything she'd heard them discussing as she came in to what Jay thought of her now that he could really see her. When she looked up, he was watching her.

"I, uh..." She didn't know what to say. Then, because she'd never been good at either subtlety or flirting, and she was going to throw up if she let herself wonder, she opened her mouth and blurted, "I really want to kiss you. I—that is, if you don't mind now that you've seen me. Maybe it's—"

"A bad idea" got cut off by the kiss. Jay took two steps and cupped her face in his hands. She was almost as tall as he was, but she was distracted enough not to worry about whether he minded. With some hesitation, she wound her arms around his neck and kissed him back. It wasn't that she hadn't done this before, but she wasn't exactly Casanova.

What were you supposed to do with your tongue while you were kissing?

Eventually, she gave up trying to think about it. For one thing, Jay didn't seem to be complaining. For another, kissing was too absorbing for her to devote much thought to anything else.

When they finally broke apart, she couldn't remember how long it had been since she had taken a breath. She stared at him. "Um."

Jay kissed her again, then groaned in frustration.

"What?" Was she doing something wrong? But when she followed his eyes, she realized the other three were outside the door staring in.

"They *did* say a moment," Jay muttered, resigned. He looked down at her. "Why did they bring you here?"

"They said they needed to figure out what Harry was up to, and since Harry had been bending the rules, maybe it was time for them to do it too." Gracie stepped back and twisted her hands together, frowning. "I know you don't always approve of that—"

"I didn't approve when it was them manipulating rankings," Jay said. "I do approve when it's keeping a crazy asshole from nuking the game." He sighed and went to open the door, gesturing with overblown courtesy for the others to come in.

"All right." The man who'd spoken up earlier seemed determined not to dwell on what they'd interrupted. "I'm Sam, Jay's boss. This is Dan, and this is Dhruv."

"Hi." Gracie brushed her fingers over her lips, blushing, and then settled down in a chair. She cleared her throat. "Um, may I have some coffee? I didn't eat on the plane."

"That's why we put all this out," Sam told her gently. "Have you slept enough to talk now? We can get you set up in one of the break rooms for a nap if you want, or take you back to your hotel—"

"No, I'm fine." Gracie managed a smile. "Honestly. Just tired." *And distracted by kissing.* She got herself a cup of coffee and a donut.

"So, I don't know how you did it," Jay said, "but you were absolutely right. It's going to be Saladin's Keep."

Gracie's head jerked up, and she stared at them. "Really?"

"We don't know that for certain," Dan pre-empted. "But it does seem like it. It also appears that he's joined forces with the Demon Syndicate. He's playing a healer."

"Yesuan," Gracie murmured.

"Ah," Dhruv said. "Of course."

"He sees himself as a healer," Gracie explained, rolling her eyes. "Unifying everyone against him, something-something." She waved the donut.

Jay laughed slightly, and she looked at him. She could still feel his lips on hers, and—

Focus, Gracie.

Gracie cleared her throat. Right. She could do this. "So, how do you know it's Saladin's Keep?" she asked.

"That's where Demon Syndicate is right now," Jay explained. "Along with a decked-out top-level healer whose account has only existed for a few days."

"So they're working with him," Gracie muttered. "Charming. Risky, though. We should ask Caspian about that."

"Good point." Jay nodded and pulled out his phone. "I'll text him."

"Whoa, wait. Hey." Dhruv made a cutting motion in the air with his hand. "Who is Caspian? We don't want to be bringing in any other people on this."

"Caspian was Demon Syndicate's plant in our guild," Gracie said. "Which I'm given to understand *you* knew about." She raised an eyebrow at him. "Now he's in our guild."

"Really." Dhruv looked at her like she was crazy. "And you…don't think this is another attempt to spy on you?"

Gracie opened her mouth, then closed it. "No," she said. "I don't. I doubt I could prove it to your satisfaction, but I really don't."

Dhruv raised an eyebrow but shrugged to show that he'd accept that for now.

"We should be watching what they're doing," Gracie said. "If Harry's there, what he's doing is our best clue."

"I've been working on getting a feed pulled up," Dan said. "Well, I asked Paul and Tim to pull one up. They just sent me a link." He plugged his laptop into a projector and clicked a few keys. "Do we want a birds-eye of the whole map or one of the players specifically?"

"Harry," Jay said at once. Gracie nodded in agreement.

They were dropped into a players'-eye view from Harry's camera. He was pacing around the greenery of the oasis, staring down at the ground.

"Interesting tactics," Gracie said, after a moment. "Think that's D or O?"

"That's about Harry's level of skill at offense," Dhruv muttered. His mouth twitched in a smile. "Seriously, though, what is he looking for?"

"I'll be back. I'm going to get my laptop." Jay headed out of the room, letting his fingertips brush Gracie's shoulder as he went past. He smiled at her when she looked at him.

She curled up to sit cross-legged in the office chair and

wrapped her fingers around the coffee mug as she stared at the screen. Harry was being very methodical, whatever he was doing. He would pace, crouch, look through the undergrowth, look up, and then repeat. Nearby, Gracie could faintly hear the sounds of spells and shouts, and once or twice, Harry looked toward the sound, but he never spent much time observing.

Jay was back less than a minute later, sliding into place beside Dan and checking several things on his screen before beginning to type furiously. Gracie glanced over curiously, but he was entirely engrossed in his work and didn't look up.

Eventually, Harry circled toward the back of the oasis, the most remote area, which was filled with larger blocks of stone and had plants everywhere. A tiny Piskie hand came up out of reflex to push the plants out of his way.

"I'll say this for him," Dhruv said. "He's finally learned how to ask other people for things."

"I don't think using other people as tools really counts as personal progress," Dan replied drily.

"You are so difficult to please."

Gracie smiled despite herself. She hadn't wanted to like these two, not after what they'd put her through. In person, though, she could see both their intelligence and their work ethic, and she found herself liking their humor. Dhruv was a straight talker, not afraid of a confrontation. Dan came at things sideways, but he had a low-key, observant way of looking at the world that Gracie liked.

She'd be lying if she said that seeing Jay wasn't one of the biggest reasons she'd come out here, but she'd also been interested in meeting the two Dragon Soul founders.

"Did they move it?" Harry muttered.

Everyone at the table stiffened, then burst out laughing. Harry was very conscious of his dignity, and hearing the Piskie voice filter was hilarious.

Unaware that they were listening in, he continued to mutter. "No, they'd take it out. But where *is* it?"

"Did we make any changes to this zone?" Dan asked quizzically. He rubbed his forehead and looked at Dhruv. "I didn't think we had."

"I didn't think we had either, but here we are." Dhruv sighed. "Wait. *Wait.* No, we flipped it. The whole thing."

"Then whatever it was would still be in the same place," Dan argued.

"Not if he tied it to a specific set of coordinates," Dhruv shot back.

Gracie looked at the two of them. She had a fairly good idea of what this meant, but she was out of her depth, and she knew it. She caught Sam's eyes and saw his empathetic smile.

"I'm lost, too," he mouthed at her and shrugged.

She smiled back.

Jay had looked up when they were speaking about flipped coordinates, and now he went back to searching with a renewed sense of purpose.

"*Ha*," he said, a moment later, causing both Gracie and Sam to start violently. He looked at them. "Sorry, but I did find something on the other side of the oasis, just in the water here." He pointed at his screen.

Gracie exchanged looks with Sam, and both of them got up to take a peek.

What was on the screen looked like gibberish to her,

but as Jay scrolled through slowly, Dan and Dhruv nodded. All three of the developers looked halfway between impressed and deeply annoyed.

"Uh." Gracie looked around. "All right, I'll ask. What am I looking at?"

"It's a challenge mechanic," Dan explained. He pointed to a few lines of code. "See, here—well, not important. It allows people to challenge one another in a way that the other person can't back out of. Of course, it only allows people to challenge who know how the mechanism works, and there are quite a few passcodes, but that's the gist. It looks like you can make it either a solo duel or a team fight."

"He's going to challenge me," Gracie said.

"We'll disable it," Dan assured her.

"Don't." Gracie crossed her arms.

Everyone turned to look at her.

"You didn't bring me out here for that," she told them. "You know as well as I do that it's this fight or another one, and another, and another. And there'd be no point to challenging me unless…"

"Unless?" Dan prompted.

The look on Jay's face told her that he, at least, knew what she meant.

"Unless it was winner-takes-all," he said quietly. "We've seen how Harry's mind works. People who don't agree with him need to be eliminated. If he wins, Gracie's gone. If *she* wins…"

Everyone looked at Gracie. She was staring down at the code with a little smile.

"Fly the rest of them out," she said. She looked at Dan

and Dhruv. "The whole guild. I want them *here* while we're fighting."

Dhruv and Dan didn't even look at each other before nodding at her.

"And since he can only summon me once I log on," Gracie said, "I'm going to go get some rest before I do."

"I'll stay here," Dan said. "I want to see if he finds it."

"He will," Dhruv predicted. "I'll have Rosalie make the arrangements for the rest of them." He paused, then said in an impressively flat tone, "Jay, would you like to take the rest of the day to show Gracie around?"

"That sounds nice," Jay agreed. "Gracie?"

"Yeah." Gracie flushed. "Yeah."

CHAPTER TWENTY-THREE

Kevin opened the door to the apartment to find a strange mix of smells: one part amazing breakfast, one part burned breakfast. He came around the doorway to the kitchen with one eyebrow raised, and his expression grew more quizzical when he saw Jamie surrounded by plates of pancakes.

"Uh, good morning."

"Jesus Christ!" Jamie practically jumped out of his skin. He'd been flipping a pancake, which flopped onto the edge of the pan and tipped onto the flames. "Oh, goddammit. *Sorry.* I was going to clean up and everything." He rescued the pancake and turned off the burner. "Uh." He cleared his throat. "You're home early."

Kevin's mouth was twitching madly. "Did you see Gracie's text?"

"No! No." Jamie looked around and patted his pockets. "I think I left my phone in the bedroom. Why, what's up?"

"They're flying all of us to Portland," Kevin said. "Everyone who can go, anyway."

"Who's 'they?'"

"Oh. Dragon Soul." Kevin raised his eyebrows. "Gracie is already there, apparently. And, well, if you think you've made enough pancakes…"

"I was trying to get them right for once!" Jamie waved his hands. His face was bright red. "Everyone should be able to make pancakes, right? It's not *hard*."

Kevin stripped off his suit jacket with a grin. "Okay, well, for one thing, most of us use a spatula to flip the pancakes, so you're doing it on hard mode. For another, we all have gaps. I, for instance, can't whistle."

"Really?" Jamie stopped, intrigued. "Seriously?"

"Seriously." Kevin smiled. "All right, text her back that you can go, we'll pack, and then we should have time for lunch before going to the airport." He looked around the kitchen at the multiple teetering stacks of pancakes. "That is, if we can find *anything* to eat."

Jamie flushed even more.

"Alan will meet us here," Kevin said. "Do you think there'll be enough pancakes for him too?"

Jamie gave him a Look and disappeared into the guest bedroom while Kevin guffawed. Then he took a bite of one of the pancakes and his expression changed. He checked to see if Jamie was watching before edging over to the trash can and spitting the mouthful out.

"Or maybe I'll buy us lunch," he called into the bedroom.

Jamie appeared in the doorway, phone in hand. "Oh, God. Are they not good?"

It took everything Kevin had to keep a straight face, and

he was pretty sure he was going to crack a rib in the process. "Man, I love you, you're great, and your cooking is generally a transcendent experience. But these are the worst pancakes I've ever had. They're both too dry and not cooked. I don't even know how you managed that."

"Ohhhh." Jamie buried his head in his hands.

"Adorable," Kevin commented.

"Huh?" Jamie's head came up.

"Nothing." Kevin headed for his own room, unbuttoning his shirt. "I'll change, then we can brainstorm lunch."

In reality, Lakhesis was Marie Wilson, a former preschool teacher turned receptionist. Her new job, as she had hoped, was less stressful.

Unfortunately, it was less stressful to the point that she was bored out of her mind. She had already redone the entire office filing system, then she had gone through it again to make new labels for everything. She had organized the supply cabinet, placed orders for anything she could think of, written a chart to show what they had, and optimized their client contact system.

She was going to go out of her mind if she had to sit here for one more minute.

Which was why, when the text message came, she gasped.

"Everything okay?" Her boss, Robert, stopped on his way across the reception area.

"Uh..." Marie looked down at the text message. "A friend just offered to fly me out for, uh...an engagement party." She bit her lip and tried to think of a good way to phrase this. "I know the next few days might be busy, so—"

"I think we're set up well," Robert said. "And I've seen how hard you've been working. It's probably a good distraction, what with...well, everything." He gave her a sad smile; she had told Robert about her sister's death. What with the funeral and the estate planning, she'd had to. Now he gave her a gentle look. "I think some time with friends would be very good for you," he told her.

Marie blinked back tears. She had expected anything other than this. Weren't bosses supposed to get on your case for asking for days off? "Thank you," she said. "Really. I, uh—"

"Why don't you take the rest of the day?" Robert suggested. "Run errands, pack, maybe go see a movie..."

"Right." Marie nodded. "I'll email you the meeting schedules for everyone, then I'll head out."

"I hope your friend has a good engagement party," Robert said sincerely.

"Mmm." She could hardly tell him what this *really* was. None of the people in her office played video games at all. "I'll pass that along. Thanks."

Ushanas pushed herself away from her desk and rolled her chair across the floor. She was riding high on the fact that she'd *finally* gotten the promotion she'd deserved for the past year and a half, and she couldn't see the day getting much better.

Well, maybe if she got a burger for lunch.

"Shannon." Taylor, one of her coworkers, popped up over the cubicle wall. "Your phone's ringing."

"Whoops, sorry." Shannon scooched her way back across the floor and picked it up. "Hello?"

"May I speak to Shannon Jeffords, please?" The voice was pleasant.

Shannon frowned. "That's me."

"Hello, Ms. Jeffords. This is Rosalie Williams at Dragon Soul Productions. As a member of Red Squadron, we're inviting you to join us tonight at the Dragon Soul Headquarters. We would be paying for your flight out."

"That's...what?" Shannon frowned at her phone.

"I understand you'll have received the details from Gracie King."

"Uh, sec." Shannon switched over to her text messages and her eyebrows shot up. Apparently, this day *was* going to get better. "Yeah, I will be able to make it." She'd be calling in sick, but that was neither here nor there. "Um, I'll wait for details from you?"

"Of course. Your email on file for your player account is the one we should use?"

"Er, yes."

"Very good. We look forward to seeing you this evening, Ms. Jeffords."

Shannon hung up and considered her desk.

"Everything okay?" Taylor called.

"Oh, yeah, that was just...my sister-in-law. She's planning my nephew's birthday party." Yeah, that hung together. Shannon pressed a hand over her stomach. "You know, I actually don't feel too well…"

"The only one we're waiting for at this point is Chowder," Gracie told Jay, "and Kevin offered to log on and see if he's there."

"Good." Jay smiled. They pushed their way out the front door into the unseasonable sunshine, and he got a sudden guilty look. "Uh…my car is a gigantic mess. Please don't judge me. You know what, maybe let's just get an Uber."

"Nuh-uh." Gracie laughed. "I wanna see. Also, where are we going?"

"Well…" Jay gave her a smile. "I'd *like* to show you all the teams and the offices, but I figured maybe that wasn't the best idea."

"Plus, we'll want everyone else to see it, too," Gracie agreed.

Jay laughed. "Dan and Dhruv are *definitely* not going to agree to that. Proprietary info and all that."

"That's a load of bullshit," Gracie told him bluntly, "what with all of the sponsored team stuff in the game."

Jay stuck out his tongue. "I didn't say it had internal logical consistency, I just said they weren't going to agree to it." He looked around. "What about this? Why don't we drop your bags off and then go get some lunch? Uh, wait, where are you staying? Did they get you a hotel, or…"

It took a moment, but Gracie caught up with his train of thought and blushed. "*Oh.* Right." She cleared her throat. "They *did* get me a hotel room, and it's pretty swanky. Let's put my bags there, and, uh…" She was really shit at flirting. "Well, if the *whole team* is going to be at the hotel, you might as well come stay with us, right?"

That was about as subtle as dropping an anvil, but Jay played along. That, or he was just as bad at this as she was. "That makes sense, yeah."

"Yeah."

"Yeah."

They both cleared their throats, and Jay fumbled with his keys to open his trunk and helped her load in her bags.

"So, is Alex coming?" He looked at her. "*Please* don't judge me for the car."

"I'm *not* going to judge you for the—are you serious?" Gracie peered in the window. "*This* is what you think of as 'super messy?' You are *never* allowed to see my car."

Jay was startled into a laugh. "Good to know."

"Anyway," Gracie said, sliding into the passenger seat, "Alex *is* coming. He's needed a vacation for a while, and he was actually able to bring Sydney with—"

Jay cut her off with a kiss. There was one moment of silence before she reached out to grab his shirt and pull him closer, and then they were making out like two teenagers in the high school parking lot, even while laughing at the absurdity of it.

When they broke away from each other, Gracie was gasping for breath. She leaned back in her seat, still laughing, and Jay did the same. She could see his heartbeat racing in his throat.

He looked at her with a grin. "That was practically torture back there in the conference room."

"I hope you never actually get tortured," Gracie said,

stifling another laugh. "You are in for a *big* surprise if you do."

"Thankfully..." Jay started the car and pulled out, "the world of video game development is not quite that intense. So, what do you want for lunch? I mean, there's obviously seafood."

"Oooh! Yes, please." Gracie settled back in her seat with a happy smile. "That's the one thing that's not good in Vegas."

"Really? *Vegas* doesn't have shellfish?"

"Oh, they do—but the good stuff is flown in, so it's all super expensive. Not like somewhere on the coast where everywhere has it."

"Good point." Jay pulled onto the highway. "So, what's it even like living in Vegas?"

"Not like you'd expect," Gracie said. "There's the Strip, obviously, but there's tons of other stuff. It's like any other city in some ways, just...full of very drunk tourists in weird outfits. It's all scandalous to them, and very normal to everyone else. Like, 'Oh hey, tits.'"

"You know, I just don't see myself getting to that point," Jay informed her blandly.

"It happens, man. Ask Alex." She grinned and curled her legs up to her chest, watching as the buildings sped by. "I feel like I should be nervous."

Jay picked up on what she meant immediately. "About Harry? And...you're not?"

"No." Gracie sighed as she stared off into the middle distance. "I'm angry. I know he might still come back someday, but I want this to be over. Dan and Dhruv? Eh, we're not going to be best friends, but I can work with them. Harry, though? He's a lunatic."

"You are not wrong." Jay shook his head. "Well, it'll be interesting to see what he's planning. And if you're not scared, then neither am I."

It wasn't here anymore. Harry's panic was rising. It *had* to be here. They could not possibly have found it; he'd hidden it too well, and in a place they would never think to look.

But he couldn't find the challenge key. It should be hovering in mid-air, ready to be used.

Ready to summon Callista.

He looked up at the sky in frustration, and that was when he noticed it. He remembered this place very well. He remembered the fall of the shadows and the way the sun had gotten in his eyes…

The sun had been on the other side of the sky when he'd been here before.

They had flipped the castle.

He looked around, mentally trying to judge where the new location of the key would be, and paced around the rim of the lake toward it. He could only hope that a flip was all that had happened. If it were more, like a flip and a shift, he might very well never find it.

He couldn't even bear to think of that.

But it was there, a faint shimmer in the air, and his breath left his lungs in a faint whoosh. Distantly, he heard Thad cursing. His team must have lost the skirmish.

Harry looked coldly toward the group.

He needed them to be on their game, and he needed

them not to ask questions about what happened to those who were lost in the Battle of Kings.

It was a war, after all. And in war, people were lost.

Forever.

CHAPTER TWENTY-FOUR

"There they are!" Gracie said excitedly, jumping up and down to look over the crowd at the arrivals gate. She held up her homemade sign, emblazoned with the words RED SQUADRON. "Mirra! Caspian! Fys!"

"Hey!" Kevin came over with a ready grin, holding out his hand for a shake.

Gracie pulled him into a hug. "Good to see you! You're taller than I expected."

"Yeah, yeah." Kevin shoved her lightly. "This is Alan." He pointed to a man in his early to mid-forties, whose light brown hair was beginning to go gray, and whose clean-cut, classic features echoed Kevin's. "And this is the baby," Kevin said, jerking his head sideways at Jamie.

Jamie rolled his eyes. "I am thirty-two." He pointed at Gracie. "*She's* the baby."

"He's right," Gracie said, but she was talking about Kevin. "You've got a baby face."

"I do not!"

"Just you wait 'til people stop carding you," Alan

advised. "Then you'll look back fondly on these days." He clapped Jamie on the shoulder. "I hope we're not staying for more than a week, by the way. I didn't want to check a bag."

"Heathen," Kevin said. He wandered toward Baggage Claim.

"Where's everyone else?" Jamie asked, falling in beside Gracie.

"Almost all here," Gracie said. "Lakhesis's plane just landed, and Chowder'll be in about an hour from now. It turns out there's a shuttle flight from San Fran."

"Chowder is from San Francisco?" Jamie asked doubtfully. "What does he do?"

"He won't say, but from the hints he dropped, he's apparently richer than God." Gracie rolled her eyes. "Which I suppose you'd have to be, to live there. Anyway, everyone else is already taking shuttles to the hotel, and we managed to get a whole block of rooms together."

"Nice," Jamie said. She noticed his gaze had wandered, however. He was staring into the distance, chewing his lip.

"Cas?" She nudged him with her elbow.

"Oh. Sorry." He looked back at her with a start, looking oddly guilty. "It's…nothing." He forced a smile. "So…how's, ah…Ushanas?"

Gracie blinked, but he didn't seem inclined to share what he was thinking. She pointed at Baggage Claim, where a woman with reddish-brown hair was standing with Alan and Kevin. "Shannon. Right over there. Seems to be doing well. I guess she pretended to be sick and is playing hooky." She felt a laugh bubbling up in her voice. "How are *you* doing? *That's* the question."

"I'm…fine." Jamie shrugged.

Gracie frowned slightly, but his face had closed off, and she didn't want to pry. She put her hands in her pockets.

"The Dragon Soul people are nice," she said finally.

Jamie nodded and made a vague noise of agreement.

Gracie took one last, curious look at him and held up her sign. "You go chill with the rest of them. I'm going to go wait for Lakhesis."

From the way he kept walking, she wasn't sure he'd even noticed her, so, with a little shake of her head, she went back to wait at the arrivals gate.

It wasn't long before they were all ensconced in the hotel. Rush hour traffic had died down and dinnertime was long since over, but Chowder insisted on buying an exorbitant amount of takeout, and presented them with—to much applause—three bottles of what appeared to be obscenely expensive alcohol.

"Oh, not tequila," Kevin said with a groan. "I can't go through that again."

"Sure, you can," Jamie told him, patting him on the arm. Gracie noticed that he still looked a little uptight and worried, and she frowned slightly. One moment, Jamie would be talking and laughing, and the next, he would look tense. What was going on with him?

Had Dhruv been right?

"You okay?" Jay asked. He hopped over the back of the couch to sit with her, and Gracie leaned into him.

"I think so," she said. Then, in a low voice, she added, "Dhruv got into my head a bit—about the newbie."

Jay went still. "Are you really worried?" he asked her. "Because I trusted your instincts when you said you believed him, and I'll trust them again if you think something's up now."

"*Something's* up," Gracie said. "But hell if I know what. I mean, he'll be fighting his own guild. It could be that, right? He's just been laid off and may or may not be having any luck job searching, so it could be that. Who knows?"

Jay wrapped his arm around her. "We could get him spectacularly drunk and see if he spills the beans."

"Not a bad idea," Gracie said speculatively. "I bet Kevin could get it out of him. They seem to get along well."

"Mmm." Jay's phone buzzed, and he reached into his pocket. He held it so they could both see the screen, and both of them scrambled upright at the same time. "Everyone stop," Jay said loudly.

Everyone froze—which was exactly what they needed, given that several people had glasses of alcohol very near their mouths. Jamie was holding his shot glass of tequila with longing, while Kevin held his with a look that spoke of a deep love-hate relationship for the stuff.

"No drinking," Gracie ordered.

"What?" Lakhesis looked down at her half-finished beer.

"No *more* drinking," Gracie clarified. "It looks like we might have to make this run tonight."

There was a stunned silence.

"Oh, hell," Chowder said.

"Double hell," Lakhesis said. She was from South Carolina, so she was three hours ahead of the rest of them. "Ohhh, this is gonna be rough. Who wants to make a coffee run with me?"

"You get a nap in," Gracie said. "At least. We'll see if we

can push it until tomorrow, okay? But people need to rest, get hydrated, and get some food into you if that's what you need. And yes, we'll have coffee for you when you wake up," she told Lakhesis."

"Right-o." The off-tank stood up. "Who'm I sharing a room with again?"

"Me." Ushanas held her hand up. "I could use some sleep, too." She handed her room key to Gracie. "Come get us when you need us, okay?"

"Will do." Gracie watched as the others drifted away, some pouring their drinks carefully back into the bottles. They had all been clustered in the main area of one of the larger suites, and as they left, she gave Jay a meaningful look.

He disappeared, and Gracie snagged Jamie.

"Hey, you got a minute?"

For a moment, she could clearly see that was the *last* thing he wanted, but he took a deep breath and gave a nod, then followed her to the main set of couches.

"You're going through a lot," Gracie said, "and I know this has to be harder on you than any of us. Fighting your old teammates, I mean."

She watched his face carefully, looking for the flicker that would betray duplicity. She didn't see it, though. He just looked sad.

"Yeah," he said. He scrubbed his hair. "It's not *Thad*, it's the rest of them. Although I suppose I'll be sad about him at some point, too."

Gracie sat back on the couch, raising one eyebrow quizzically. "I thought he was a douche of the highest order."

That got a laugh out of Jamie. "He definitely can be." The man settled back on the couch. "It was my whole community, you know? I got to thirty and didn't have a girlfriend…" He looked troubled, then shook his head. "I just never built anything, you know? And it was easier to ignore that when I was getting paid to play video games all day. I told myself I'd made it, that was the dream. Now I don't have that anymore."

Gracie nodded. "I know how that feels," she offered.

"You're, ah…you're *one* year out of college?" Jamie asked, raising an eyebrow.

"I may not be as old as you," Gracie said, nettled, "but I *do* get what it's like to feel like you're on the wrong track and the 'right' track is still somewhere you don't want to be."

Jamie gave her a look of appreciation. "That's actually… a really good way to put it. I feel like I should have built something by now—you know, have a house, a wife, kids." Again, he looked uncomfortable. "But I don't want that. It just feels like losing *not* to have it?"

"Yeah." Gracie nodded. "No, I totally get that. I'm supposed to be in grad school or working for some Fortune 500 company, dating a preppy guy on the management track, getting ready for that same whole schtick—marriage, kids, pretty Christmas cards."

Jamie laughed. "You don't look like you want it any more than I do."

"Yeah." Gracie shrugged. "That's the way of it, huh? And that's the problem with charting your own course. You know you don't want to go the way people are telling you to go, but that doesn't tell you anything about what you're actually going for. It's all uncharted territory."

"Yeah," Jamie said, with feeling. "Yeah," he added again, quietly. "Yeah, that's about the way of it."

"Jamie…" Gracie shook her head. "Cas. Sorry, I can't call you anything but Cas."

He gave her a tired smile.

"Are you *okay?*" Gracie asked. "You look happy, and then you look so sad."

She had said the wrong thing. Jamie's face closed off entirely. He swallowed.

"It's nothing," he said finally. "Really. Honestly."

Yeah, that sounds real. But Gracie knew better than to say that. Humor wasn't going to make him feel any better, so she bit her lip and nodded. "Sure. Well, glad to hear it."

"Yeah." Jamie stood. "I should get some sleep."

He left without another word, and when the door had closed, Jay came out into the main room with a speculative look on his face.

"Any idea what that was about?"

"Not the first thought," Gracie said, troubled. She got up and began to put away the boxes of takeout food. There wasn't much left, but it might make a good snack for someone later.

Plus, it gave her something to do.

Jay came to help her in silence, so they were both working when there was a knock at the door. Jay went to get it and came back with Dan and Dhruv at his heels.

"Hey," Gracie said, looking up. Then she saw their expressions. "What's wrong?"

To her surprise, it was Dan who answered, his tone

direct. "It's not just *you* who'll be fighting winner-takes-all," he said flatly. "Anyone who dies in the fight, and anyone who's on the losing team? They're out of the game too. Forever."

There was a pause, and then Gracie said simply, "No."

Dan and Dhruv exchanged looks.

"There could be benefits," Dan said quietly. "As you mentioned, this is a way to get Harry out of the game."

"No. Collateral. Damage." Gracie shook her head. "I didn't fly these people out here for the possibility that they'd never be part of the game again, and—" She broke off and swallowed. "Even the Demon Syndicate doesn't deserve this."

"They probably don't know," Jay said. When everyone looked at him, he shrugged. "Come on, you think the whole guild just decided, 'Hey, let's take the chance of getting banned from the game forever'?"

Gracie nodded. It was a good point. They probably *didn't* know.

"Okay," she said. "Well, it's even more important, then. They literally don't know it's life or death."

"If we take that part out," Dan said, "it means Harry won't get banned. There won't be any reason to go through with this."

"Find a way," Gracie said bluntly.

"Now, wait a second," Jay argued. "If it's winner-takes-all, even for you two, that means there's a chance that *you*—"

"I know." Gracie looked at him. "I do. But that's what monarchs *are*, Jay. What leaders are. They're the ones who do the things that…" She swallowed. "They stand in the way," she said. "And they take the risks."

Dan waited, his gaze assessing both of them. Even Dhruv was uncharacteristically quiet.

Gracie tried to smile. "If we don't take him out now, it's just going to keep going like this forever—new ways, new cheat codes, new hacks. As long as we don't deal with him, he's going to hold the game back. Enough." She looked at Dan. "Also, I'm a big believer in poetic justice. His quest should be how he gets shut out of the game. Just figure it out so the teams are safe."

Dan gave a nod. "I'll do what I can. No one from your team is to log on until I do. We'll push a server update and tell you when it's done."

CHAPTER TWENTY-FIVE

"Your warrior is a problem," Yesuan said bluntly to Thad later. "His DPS isn't up to par, and he's easily distracted. He took too many runs to get a rhythm down for getting across the oasis."

"And?" Thad asked.

Yesuan gave him a look.

They were standing in the oasis by moonlight. The rest of the guild had teleported home; only Yesuan and Thad were left. Birds called in the night, and the wind in the trees and shifting moonlight lent an eerie feel to the place.

It was easy to see how ghost stories had gotten started. Even knowing that none of the people involved were real, Thad found himself wondering why this keep was abandoned.

Yesuan said nothing, so Thad dragged his thoughts back to the matter at hand.

"You wanted us to run the scenario within certain parameters," he said. "We did." He shrugged. "Our acquaintance is likely to be brief. Why does it matter to you now if it took too many runs for Grok to come up to par?"

"You don't care about quality?" Yesuan asked.

Thad's temper broke. "I don't care if you're happy with my guild, beyond the very simple metric of whether or not we completed your task. You wanted results, and that's what you'll get."

Yesuan looked at the lake. Thad followed his eyes and spotted a small shimmer in the air. Was he imagining it?

No. Yesuan had been looking at it this whole time. Interesting.

"Why are you even here?" Thad asked.

Yesuan gave him another look.

"I think I deserve an answer," Thad said, "if you can't do this without us."

"No." Yesuan sounded bored. "You don't. You deserve what you bargained for, which was to win the next Month First you run."

Thad was done with this. "Fine. Then maybe I don't like the bargain. Maybe I walk."

Yesuan rounded on him. It was ridiculous to see from a Piskie, and Thad laughed. That was the wrong choice, however.

"You have nothing if you walk away," Yesuan spat at him. "Brightstar will decide to oust you to convince their investors they're making a good return, your team will crumble, and people will remember you as the figurehead of a doomed experiment."

"You're so ridiculous!" Thad clenched his hands and tried not to scream. "You are *insane*! Everything is a matter of life and death to you!"

"Everything *is* a matter of life and death," Yesuan hissed. "No decision comes without hurting someone, no wrongdoing or failure is without cost. *You* are sloppy. You care about your own prestige at the cost of everything else. You are—" He broke off and turned away.

Thad stood frozen, shaking. "I am *what*?" he asked finally. "What am I?"

Yesuan said nothing for a long time. His character was so still, in fact, that Thad wondered if he had disconnected.

"You are someone who has much to achieve," Yesuan said. He sounded almost like he was reciting something. "With your *guidance*, your team could achieve so much more. Isn't that what you want to show your sponsors? Isn't that the team you promised them?"

Thad frowned. This was so much nicer than Yesuan's words had been before. It seemed out of place with the rest of the conversation.

But his pride swelled up at that. Perhaps Yesuan was right. Thad *had* been preoccupied with his own ranking, with snapping orders. But the team looked up to him. Perhaps, if he were to make each of them feel as though he truly cared, as though they were a special piece of the Demon Syndicate—

That sounded exhausting, and he rolled his eyes in the real world.

But perhaps it would work. The team would come together, they would win the Month First, and when Yesuan left, they would attract another healer easily.

Their conversation was interrupted by a bright purple message that flashed across the screen.

SERVER MAINTENANCE IN 2:00

SERVER MAINTENANCE IN 1:59
SERVER MAINTENANCE IN 1:58

"What the hell?" Yesuan spat. His caring tone was gone in an instant. "What do they know? What are they doing?"

"What do you mean?" Thad's face settled into a frown. Something about this seemed…off.

Yesuan was cursing. "The challenge against Callista. She'll be called here when she logs on, which has been *far* longer than it should have been, and now unexpected maintenance? They know something."

"Who is *they*?" Thad demanded.

Yesuan ignored him. "Would they help her? No. And they haven't banned this account—"

"What are we doing?" Thad asked suddenly. "Will they ban our accounts for this?"

Yesuan gave him a look. "No," he said very precisely, in a way that was somehow not reassuring at all. "They will not. Keep your team ready. If this is really unconnected to everything else, I want them all online and ready as soon as the servers come back up. We need to be ready."

"I didn't know it was going to be tonight—"

Yesuan had run across the oasis, and now he was doing something complicated by the shimmering patch of air. "We'll have to hope it's enough," he said to himself. To Thad, he said, "Yes, tonight. The longer we give her to prepare, the more dangerous she'll be."

Dan settled back in his chair. "I don't like this."

"Why not?" Dhruv shrugged. "It's very low-risk from our end."

"What if she loses?" Dan demanded.

Dhruv stared at him for a long moment. "Then we find another way to deal with him." His eyes focused over Dan's shoulder on the progress flashing across the screen as the update pushed to the servers. "I don't see the problem."

"If she loses, she'll be gone." Dan didn't seem happy with his explanation, but neither did he offer another one.

Dhruv frowned, and then took a chair. He leaned his elbows on his knees. "So, now you don't *want* her gone? Because I'd think it would be a nice, tidy solution."

"It would leave us with Harry, but *without* the one person who might have been a check on him."

"We pull the servers down if she loses, then, and remove the first stage of the quest." Dhruv shrugged.

"It's already removed in this update." Dan gave a tight smile. "No one else can get at it, I made sure of that."

"Well, aren't you clever?" Dhruv sat back. "So what's the problem? Honestly?"

Dan thought about it. He went over to the mini fridge in the corner and took out one of the bottled waters he drank. Dan only drank one brand of bottled water, and no one else in the office was allowed to touch his mini-fridge on pain of death.

He sat back down and stared at the screen for a while, tracking progress.

"I'd feel bad for her if she was thrown out of the game because she got caught up in someone else's fight," he said finally. "That wouldn't be fair."

Dhruv gave a shrug. "Nothing's fair. Or...there's always the chance. It's the price you pay for being alive. Life is full of random chance."

"Yes, but since we're in charge of this one, shouldn't we *try* to make it fair?" Dan demanded. "Shouldn't we?"

Dhruv opened his mouth, then waved his hands and sat back in his chair moodily.

"Yeah," Dan said. "Exactly."

"You know, you could have just kept that to yourself." Dhruv picked at an imaginary speck of dust on his pants.

"Rather than trouble your delicate conscience?" Dan asked sweetly. He took a sip of water.

Dhruv glared at him. "You know what I meant."

"Yes, I just said it." Dan raised his eyebrows. "So, what do we do?"

There was a long pause while Dhruv looked into the middle distance with a surly expression. Then he smiled.

"We do what Harry would do," he said.

Harry stared at the webpage, unblinking. It had been twenty minutes since the servers went down, and it might be hours.

But if he missed this, if he was offline when Callista logged on, he didn't know what would happen to the challenge. If she had a chance to prepare, or log out and make a new character, or—

There was no knowing what she would do. He had meant what he said to Thad: Callista was dangerous.

His lip curled. Thad was a fool. By now, any reasonable person should have seen that Harry had no intentions of following through on his end of the bargain. He wouldn't have to if Thad died, and his help would hardly matter if most of Thad's team was lost.

And it would be. Players never expected death in a video game to be permanent. They would run headlong into danger without a thought. It would be a valuable lesson for everyone else.

If, of course, the challenge still existed. He wanted to snarl. To come so close, only to have the opportunity yanked away now.

Because there was nothing left. If he lost this, if he wasn't able to bring Callista down and take the crown that way, there was no further recourse. The very thought of losing made his blood turn icy.

He told himself that it was impossible for him to lose. This quest had been made for him, *by* him, as an expression of reality.

He was meant to have it.

The server light blinked green, and his throat caught. He texted Thad with shaking fingers and went to get his VR headset on. He was about to find out if all of his work had been undone.

But when he logged on, the challenge still showed in the corner of his screen, unanswered and unclaimed.

Harry sagged in relief. He was meant to win this, he told himself. He was born for this—to be this king, in this era, in this world. That was why he was here.

He created a party and ordered them to get ready.

Almost, he told them to pray. For many, this was the last fight of their time here. That deserved some sort of recognition. But he said nothing, in the end.

Some people were born to be pawns.

CHAPTER TWENTY-SIX

The map on the table was printed out on glossy paper, far superior to anything Gracie could have drawn on her own. She had to admit that.

On the other hand, she had a soft spot for maps hand-drawn on sheets of taped-together graph paper. It was how she'd built the earliest worlds she played in, and it was how she still liked to organize her thoughts.

Regardless, this was what they had: a custom-made board to plan their strategy in Saladin's Keep. Rosalie, the receptionist at Dragon Soul, had come over to the hotel with all of the materials. She had remembered every single one of their names and inquired as to relevant details of each person's flight.

Gracie would bet good money that Rosalie would be running some company or other within the next few years if she wanted to.

Gracie planted her hands on the map and looked down.

"The east hallway is better if they don't know we're there," Ushanas said. She crossed her arms over her chest.

"There are more places to hide that are invisible from both ends of the corridor, so we can set up ambushes that just keep going. They think they've gotten away from one, then they run into another one. Their team comes to help, and *they* get ambushed."

Gracie nodded.

"But there's no flag," Dathok clarified. "Right?" Of all of them, he almost resembled his character. He was tall, with incredibly broad shoulders and decisive features.

"No flag," Gracie confirmed. "Just a weird sort of battle royale. Anyone on a team can attack the other team's leader, and if either leader dies…" She met Jay's eyes across the table. "The fight is over," she finished.

Jay opened his mouth to speak, but she cut him off with a tiny shake of her head. She didn't want anyone on the team to know the stakes. She wanted them to go into this fight with their heads on straight and their focus razor-sharp. She didn't want them worrying.

Alex had clearly noticed what had passed between them, but he said nothing. His girlfriend, Sydney, was curled up on the other side of the room with a book and was slowly falling asleep.

Kevin was tapping his fingers on the side of his face as he stared down at the map. He and Alan had been murmuring together, and Gracie remembered that they'd been playing video games together for years.

Her heart ached at the idea of having a sibling she was that close with. She looked around the table and saw Jamie watching them, his face drawn. She frowned and kept scanning. Freon was about as unremarkable a person as it was possible to be, with the sort of face you forgot very easily. He should, Gracie thought vaguely, be a spy. Lakhesis had curly brown hair that was escaping the multitude of clips and hair ties she had used, and a smile that always had an edge of sadness to it.

Gracie looked down at her phone when it buzzed. It was a message from Dhruv, telling her that the servers were online, Harry was online, and—

She frowned.

"All right, get ready to go, people. We're getting a shuttle over to the building."

Alex went over to kneel by the couch. Gracie heard him say something to Sydney, and she murmured something back sleepily. Her hand emerged from her blanket to clasp his, and Gracie made out the words, "Good luck."

She smiled. When Alex looked at Sydney, his whole face softened. Gracie had known on some level that he was missing something, but she hadn't realized just how much happier he could be.

So she was smiling when she came out into the hall and saw Jay waiting for her. She took his hand as they walked and saw his curious expression.

"Dhruv says they have something for me," she said, with a shrug. "I don't know what that means." She tapped the rolled-up map against her leg with the other hand. "Shot glass of arsenic, maybe?"

Jay snorted. "If they had one of those, it would be for Harry."

"That's true. Good point." She squeezed his hand. "Jay?"

"Yeah?"

"I'm scared." The words came out before she could stop

them. She squeezed her eyes shut, and when his arms came around her, tears leaked out. "I'm so scared."

"So don't do it," Jay said urgently. He cupped her face in both hands, his eyes searching hers. "Gracie, *don't*. They said they could make it so no one was out of the game. Dan wanted to. You don't have to put yourself in danger for this."

Gracie tried to laugh, but it sounded like a sob. "You know that isn't an answer. It still leaves us with the problem—"

"You don't have to solve the problem!" Jay's voice rose. He was furious, but not with her. "It was never yours to solve. You weren't supposed to be caught up in this. Harry's an asshole who couldn't—"

She put her hand on his chest, and he broke off. She gathered her courage to speak, trying her hardest not to start crying.

She *hated* crying. She decided to be angry at Harry for making her cry.

That helped her get her bearings.

"You don't always get to choose what you get caught up in," Gracie stated. "That's life, Jay. All you get to choose is what you do with that."

"I know," Jay said, "but Gracie—"

Gracie shook her head and put her fingers over his mouth. "You fought so hard to get me through that quest," she said. "When I wanted to give it up, you told me you thought I deserved it. I doubted myself, but you never doubted me. You went to Sam and asked for his help so we could get through the run before the servers went down. *Why?*"

Jay didn't immediately answer when she took her fingers away. His eyes searched hers. "Because I thought you would be a good queen," he said finally. He shook his head helplessly. "I thought Harry was…" He sighed and looked away. "Fundamentally misguided," he finished finally. He looked back at her. "I believe the way he sees the world is wrong, but he set up a test that you passed for the *right* reasons. You cared about the world. You wanted to do the right thing."

Gracie nodded, smiling sadly.

Jay realized what she meant a moment later. "No. No, Gracie, please! If you use that to justify putting yourself in danger, I'll never forgive myself."

"You didn't make it true by saying it," Gracie pointed out. "A good leader doesn't throw other people into danger instead of themselves. A good tank *certainly* doesn't. Jay, I want to be a good leader. I'm taking the risk because this best-case scenario is the better one. Nothing ventured, nothing gained."

Jay's fingers clenched. "If we lose you—"

"If you lose me, *Metamorphosis* will still be what it was—and you will not for a second let Harry win forever." Gracie reached up to lay her hand on his cheek. "I know that. He may be a crazy bastard, but he was right about one thing: people will come together to defeat a tyrant."

Jay sighed. "Do me a favor?"

"Sure," Gracie said cautiously.

Jay kissed her, his eyes closing for a long moment, and when he pulled away, he laid his forehead against hers and met her eyes. "*Win*," he said.

Gracie laughed. She couldn't help it. She laughed and

wrapped her arms around him and held on tight while he hugged her back.

"Just a little favor, huh?" she asked.

"Uh-huh." Jay wrapped his arm around her, and they kept walking. He sounded smug.

Gracie's phone buzzed, and she pulled it out of her sweatshirt before groaning and showing the screen to Jay.

Stop canoodling, Alex had texted. **Alan is teaching people sea shanties and I'm going out of my mind.**

It was only a few minutes later that they pulled into the parking lot of Dragon Soul Productions and piled out. Most of the lights were off, and Dan was waiting for them in the lobby so that the sleepy night shift of security guards wouldn't be overwhelmed.

When they got up to the main level, Dan pointed down the hallway. "Dhruv is waiting for you that way," he told Gracie. "I'll get everyone else hooked up and your account prepped."

"Thanks," Gracie said. She squeezed Jay's hand and headed off curiously to stick her head in the door of the only office with lights on. "Hello?"

"Hi." Dhruv beckoned her over. "Your character is where?"

"The temple ruins outside Kithara," Gracie said.

"All right, I'll head there." Dhruv was remotely piloting a character.

"You can play that way?" Gracie asked, surprised.

"Eh, it's a bit buggy as an interface, but yeah. Made it a lot easier to test certain things." Dhruv set his character to auto-run and brought up his inventory. "Harry's challenge brings the two leaders to the same stats once the battle starts—same crit chance, same damage modifier, same hit points."

Gracie sighed and nodded.

"It *doesn't* work, though," Dhruv said smugly, "on any future changes."

"Eh?" Gracie frowned down at him. She was beginning to wish she'd had some coffee when Lakhesis did.

Dhruv, seeing her gaze light on his coffee cup, handed it up to her without comment. "If you switch your armor and weapon *after* the battle starts, you'll gain an advantage," he explained.

"That's cheating," Gracie said, shocked. "The whole point of this was that—"

"Fuck that," Dhruv said. "You can bet your ass that Harry's planned some dirty trick or other. Hell, this whole thing was a dirty trick. He never intended this to be fair. He only wanted it to be fair if he won, and if he didn't win, he'd keep stacking the deck until he did. He wanted to be a dictator. I don't want that, and neither do you."

Gracie swallowed.

"This armor will bring you back to the stats you *should* have had with the armor and weapon you have now," Dhruv said. "If I thought I could give you infinite hit points and a hundred percent crit and you'd take it, I would have done that. But you wouldn't, would you?"

"No," Gracie said at once.

"You know," Dhruv told her, "there's a very large overlap between honorable and stupid."

Gracie gave him a look. "Will that be all?"

"Yes. I'll meet you there when you get online and trade you the armor. You should have ten minutes or so to prepare before you get ported to the challenge area." Dhruv looked at her. "You ready?"

"As ready as I'm gonna be," Gracie said.

He raised an eyebrow. "Are you or aren't you?"

Gracie looked at the screen. She didn't have to use the armor, she told herself. She could choose.

And she had beaten Harry before. She would do it again.

"I'm ready," she told him.

CHAPTER TWENTY-SEVEN

Gracie had barely joined the party and completed the trade with Dhruv's character before the challenge yanked them all through the ether to Saladin's Keep.

It was night there too, with moonlight catching on drifting dust in the library and illuminating the wreckage. Saladin had entertained even the most heretical scholars, keeping books on necromancy, demon summonings, atheism, new medical techniques, and more.

In the end, a mob had come for him with a challenger at its head. Surrounded by their most elite guards, they had fought.

Saladin had lost.

This was indeed the place where unworthy kings fell.

Gracie was not unworthy. She told herself that, although her chest was tight and her heart was pounding. On neutral ground lit up gold, she approached Harry for one last conversation. It was hard to take him seriously as a Piskie, but she knew better than to underestimate him.

Dhruv was right. Harry would cheat if he could.

"You took something that wasn't yours," Harry said. "You don't deserve it. I will take it back tonight."

Gracie looked at him for a long time. She remembered his face when he had come to her apartment—desperate, anguished. "You dreamed a better king than you could have been," she said quietly. "And for that, I thank you."

She turned on her heel and left without another word, returning to her team in the library. Harry did not call her back, but she felt his anger and pain following her.

You made yourself into someone who needed to be destroyed, Gracie thought. *You wrote the Yesuan quest, and somehow thought it would end differently for you.*

In the library, with the counter at two minutes, she looked at all of them and sighed. "Boy, did you all get more than you bargained for in this game!"

Everyone burst out laughing.

"Some of you have been here right from the start and some haven't," Gracie said, "but every one of you has been there to watch the weird-ass clusterfuck of this quest. I kind of hoped we were done with that bullshit now. Apparently not." She did jazz hands.

"Nothing worthwhile is ever that easy," Kevin chimed in.

Gracie smiled at him. "I just wanted to say, I appreciate more than I can say that each one of you is here, and that it is *you guys* who are here. I couldn't have asked for a better group—Dathok to talk lore with, Lakhesis to tank with, Mirra to train new healers, Fys to take notes and make data-driven suggestions, Ushanas to tell me to get my head out of my ass…"

Ushanas chuckled.

"Every one of you has been there for me and for each other," Gracie said. "I just—thank you." If she said anything more, her voice was going to start shaking and they were going to know something was wrong. "Fuck 'em up," she finished with a laugh.

"Red Squadron!" Chowder said.

"Red Squadron!" Everyone chorused back.

Gracie turned to Jay. There was so, so much more he'd done than she could ever fit in a speech, and she hoped he knew that. He nodded slightly and reached out for a fist-bump.

Gracie took a deep breath and let it out slowly. Thirty seconds now. Her heart rate was increasing.

You can do this, she told herself. *Don't fuck up.* As the counter entered single digits, all of her attention focused on the main door, and on what she knew of her opponent.

What she didn't notice was Caspian waiting by one of the side doors, only to slip out as soon as the counter hit zero and the screen announced CHALLENGE STARTED.

The counter flashed and disappeared as the doors opened. Harry watched as the team charged out into the oasis, leaving a carefully-selected team of rogues and mages to watch him.

He waited for the explosion of communication, the calls between the teammates as they herded opponents into place and warned one another of sneak attacks. He had warned them that deaths in this battleground were permanent.

He had failed to mention just *how* permanent, of course.

The calls, however, didn't begin. Harry sank into the shadows and waited, a frown on his face.

"Grok," Thad said, his voice very low. "Report."

"No one," Grok replied.

"Scan the roofs," Thad ordered. "Don't give into the temptation to seek them out. Be patient; make them come to us."

Harry nodded. Thad might be limited by his pride, but he had a good tactical mind. He wouldn't throw players away to no purpose in this confrontation.

He didn't stop scanning the darkness, though. Something was coming.

There was no way Callista had come here without a plan.

Thad crouched in the shadow of one of the trees and narrowed his eyes. Callista's team should be here. There was *no* way they had beat Thad's team to the oasis since there had been eyes on the other door, and they'd timed the runs from both sides. The great hall was closer to the oasis than the library was, by several crucial yards.

Which meant they were in the hallways.

Thad wanted to smile. On the one hand, that was idiotic. Everyone knew the fastest way through the keep was via the oasis.

On the other hand, if Callista was determined to wait them out, she actually *might* win at forcing them into the hallways.

Thad ground his teeth.

"Preacher."

"Yeah?"

"I want you to scout. Do *not* engage. I want to know how they're set up in those corridors so we can pick them off one by one."

"They'll have to come out eventually," Yesuan objected. "You were right the first time. Make them come to us."

"You don't know Callista well, do you?" Thad asked. "I suppose I'm not surprised, given how badly she got under your skin just now." No one but the two leaders had been at the first meeting, but they had all noticed Yesuan's clipped responses when he came back to the great hall. Whatever Callista had said to him, it had been the last thing he wanted to hear.

Yesuan's stony silence was enough to give Thad a deep sense of satisfaction.

"She will absolutely be more patient than us," Thad said. "She will wait as long as she needs to."

"Then so will we," Yesuan snapped back. "I will not lose because her team was better disciplined than my own."

"What if you lose because there's an entire group of them massing to take the great hall in a rush?" Thad asked bluntly.

Nothing.

"Preacher, go check."

"Will do." Preacher, at least, did not seem inclined to take Yesuan's orders over Thad's. That was something.

Thad felt a swell of pride as he saw the rogue's stealthed shimmer go past the main door, creeping toward one of the corridors. Callista's team was *not* better disciplined than his, nor did they have the training. They didn't know shorthand or have a cohesive idea of which side of the battlefield was left or right since they hadn't trained on dozens of maneuvers and formations.

There was no way she would win this.

He waited. In some battlegrounds, stealth was paramount, which meant that someone's voice chat could be heard by the other team if they were close enough. Not knowing the specific rules here, Thad had ordered his team not to speak unless they could be sure they were alone.

When he heard the rustle behind him, he thought Preacher had come back, and he turned with a questioning tilt to his head.

But it wasn't Preacher. It was Jamie.

Jamie had left as soon as the doors were open. He had told Jay's team in the east hall that he would be with Lakhesis' group, and after he got to the end of the western hallway, he waited and slipped around to the other oasis entrance.

Despite what Gracie had considered to be extensive preparations, no one was watching out for each other, ready to send her a private message that someone else was out of position. They would simply assume that Jamie had a good reason for being somewhere else.

Which, in his own way, he did.

He'd thought a lot on the flight out about how this battleground was going to be structured, and he'd come to two inescapable conclusions.

And Thad needed to know about them.

When Thad turned around, Jamie saw the surprise in the set of his shoulders and the way he took a step back. Thad reached for his weapon as Jamie held his hands up. Now that he thought of it, all of this hinged on whether he could open a private channel to one of the enemy team, but he had bet he'd be able to.

After all, Harry had wanted this to be as much like real combat as possible.

"I'm not here to attack you," Jamie said.

"You're a healer," Thad shot back, his voice dripping condescension. "What do you think you'd be able to do?"

"That *should*," Jamie said patiently, "prove my sincerity. Right?"

After a pause, Thad shrugged. "Then why are you here?"

"To explain the rules of the battleground," Jamie said. "If you die in this battleground, you die." He waited. "You're out of the game."

There was a pause while Thad stared at him.

"You're wrong," he said finally.

"I'm not." Jamie shook his head. He looked over his shoulder to where the rustle of bushes said that someone was sneaking up on him. "I came here to tell you this, because…I left, but you don't deserve to be out of the *game* for someone else's fight. There's no way that's all right."

Thad gave a tight laugh. "You want me to believe that you have my best interests at heart? *You?*"

"No." Jamie shook his head. "I want you to believe that I care enough about all of you that I'm willing to take a risk to keep you from getting banned. *That's* what I want you to believe. Is that so impossible for you?"

Thad hesitated, and Jamie knew what he was thinking. Thad liked to think in terms of black and white—Jamie wasn't on his team anymore, so he was enemy, someone to hate. But deep down, Thad knew things were more complicated than that.

"You're telling me Callista *told* you that was the case?" Thad asked finally.

"Yes." Jamie didn't waver. "There aren't…a lot of us here." He could feel Thad's smile. "And I know that seems like a good opening, but is it worth it if one of you gets thrown out? If it's *you*, Thad?"

Thad hesitated now and turned away.

"You could be lying," he said.

"I could be, but I'm not." Jamie looked at him steadily. "And I told them I'd play lookout, so if you want to retreat, if you want to leave, *whatever* you want to do, I'll cover for you. Do it however you want so that you can trust me."

Thad stepped closer. "Why shouldn't I just kill *you*?" he asked. "You left. I might lose my job because of you. You stabbed me in the back."

Jamie had known it might come to this. His heart was pounding now. "You shouldn't kill me for the same reason I came to warn you." He kept his voice low. He caught Thad's tiny gesture for whoever was sneaking up on him to wait and took courage from that. "We're not on the same team anymore, but you know there's more to it than that. I'll always be grateful to you. I'll always try to shield you from things like this." He swallowed. "I hope you'd do the same for me."

Thad said nothing. He looked around the oasis, and Jamie wondered if he had switched to the main channel. There was a long pause.

Then he nodded. Jamie hadn't expected him to be able to vocalize this, so he wasn't surprised. Thad turned and walked away, some of the others trailing him, and Jamie melted into the shadows.

"Guys?" Gracie's voice was suddenly worried. "They're leaving the battle. What's going on?"

"I told them the truth," Jamie said. At last, he allowed himself to smile. "Well, I told them part of the truth."

"Jamie." Gracie's voice was very pleasant and bland. "What did you say?"

"Well, I was doing some thinking," Jamie said. Now that the adrenaline rush was over, it was all he could do not to laugh hysterically. He was shaking. "Harry meant this as a way to get his crown back—or challenge whoever had it. He is a very might-makes-right type of person."

"Maybe we should discuss this after—"

"Which meant he set it up so whoever lost was gone. Forever." Jamie knew she hadn't wanted him to say those words, but he wasn't going to hold back. "And he wanted it to be like real warfare. He wanted to measure a king by who would die for them, so those rules applied to us, too."

"I would never—" Her voice was urgent.

"I know," Jamie said. "I know you wouldn't. I knew you would *never* allow us to go into that kind of danger. The servers went down tonight. You made them change it, didn't you?"

"Yes," Gracie said. "Look, it wasn't important. You were all going to be okay, so—"

"But *you're* still on the line," Jamie said. He knew what she'd been trying to do, and he wasn't going to let her. None of them would forgive themselves if they made a stupid mistake and Gracie was gone forever. "There had to be stakes, or we wouldn't be here. You want to get rid of Harry, so you left in one part: whichever team leader loses, they *are* gone."

There was silence.

"Gracie?" Kevin's voice was hushed.

"He's wrong," Lakhesis said. "Isn't he?"

"He's right," Jay asserted.

"Jay—" Gracie sounded desperate.

"He is," Jay said. "And it's right for them to know. Didn't you want to be different from Harry? You're not sacrificing them, but you're also not telling them the whole truth."

Silence.

"He lied to them," Gracie said finally. "We won't win honorably."

"No," Jamie said. "Because none of them were willing to die for him. That's why they're leaving. He lied to them and used them. Yeah, I might not have told them that the rules had changed, but I was honest about what he was planning."

Gracie groaned and then started to laugh. "How many are left?"

"A few." Jamie frowned. "Thad. Preacher—he's a rogue. Harkness, an ice mage. And Grok, actually. He never got on with Thad, so I wonder why— Oh, hell. Thad didn't tell him. Bastard."

"Delightful," Gracie said. Privately, she added, "You could have *asked* me, you know."

"You would have said no," Jamie said simply.

"Well, yes."

"Yeah. So I didn't ask." He smiled lazily, went to lean on the wall, and nearly overbalanced in the real world.

There were occasional problems with immersive games.

"*This* was why you were so out of it?" Gracie pressed. "You were worried that I might sacrifice you all?"

Jamie felt his gut twist. "Uh, not exactly. Look, let's just get through this. We'll talk about that later."

"Sure." He could feel her curiosity. "All right, team, Jamie's given us a better playing field, but we know Harry's a lying, egotistical son of a bitch. Stay on your toes, and let's see which way he's planning to cheat next."

They were gone. One by one, they were logging out.

"Thad. *Thad.*" Harry's voice was tight with fury.

There was no answer.

That meant he had one choice left. In the darkness, the healer's eyes began to glow red. Teeth lengthened, claws sprouted, and the bright pink Piskie hair went black.

If ever there had been a time and place for a demonic transformation, Saladin's Keep tonight was it.

CHAPTER TWENTY-EIGHT

"All right," Gracie told her team. "Stay where you are, keep communicating, and keep your eyes open. When in doubt, try to slow down the pace of the fight. Kite him, snare him, stun him. Well...and any of the others you see."

"There's a definite chance he's getting reamed out by Thad right now," Jamie chimed in.

The strangled noise that followed that pronouncement sounded like it came from Kevin.

Then, "Gracie." It was Jamie. "There's, uh...he's in the oasis, and he's a fucking demon."

"Everyone *stay where you are.*" Gracie headed for the oasis, her crowd-control team at her heels, then skidded to a halt. *You're gonna cheat, you bastard? Well, you're not the only one with hidden powers.* She switched into her other set of armor and grabbed her new weapon and watched her stats climb in satisfaction.

There was a yell from Jamie, inarticulate, and a few people called out.

"Stay where you are!" Gracie yelled again. "We're on our way!"

She burst out into the oasis in a storm of both fireballs and ice; Ushanas and Freon made an incredible duo when it came to distractions. From the way Harry's character stopped and wavered, she knew they'd made a strong opening.

He was, however, freaky as hell. For one thing, he could fly now. For another, he looked like someone had transformed a Piskie into something halfway between a werewolf and a vampire with glowing red eyes.

Gracie swung her shield out, hefted her axe, and stared at him. "So," she called. "You decided you'd stack the deck in case you couldn't win in a fair fight, huh?"

"And you decided to take my team!" Harry roared back. "What the hell did you do? You *dare* accuse *me* of cheating?"

"She didn't get rid of them," Jamie called, sending a low-level DoT spell at Harry's circling form. "I did. I made a bet you wouldn't tell them any death was permanent, and it looks like I was right."

Harry's head whipped around.

"And Gracie told you?"

"Yes," Jamie called back, lying with impressive conviction. "And we all signed up anyway."

Harry leveled a blast of purple-black flames at Jamie and the healer's form crumpled to the ground.

"If you want to die," Harry said, "then die."

Gracie felt a rush of white-hot rage. Jamie wasn't going to be out of the game forever, but Harry didn't know that. He'd done something immeasurably cruel just because he could. Out of spite.

"Ushanas. Freon."

"On it, boss."

Ice spears appeared, sticking out of Harry's body as fire exploded across his skin. His health bar took a hit, and he tumbled toward the ground...

Only to crouch over Jamie's body. His health bar went back up, and Jamie's character rose jerkily. He ran at Gracie like a zombie and began battering at her shield.

"This is *not me!*" Jamie called.

"I know, man," Gracie said. "And, uh, I'm sorry for what I'm about to do. Maybe close your eyes?"

"Can do."

Gracie swung the shield and whirled to bring the axe down in a heavy chop. Jamie's zombie body went staggering sideways and then rounded on her with a snarl. Roots appeared out of nowhere, snagging him in place while Gracie threw her shield at Harry.

He might be able to feast on corpses and level people with a single blast of flame, but he couldn't escape direct hits. He went down, stunned, and Gracie piled on with a sudden influx of warriors and rogues.

"I thought I told you guys to stay put."

"Did you?" Jay asked innocently. "I must have missed that."

There was a zombie noise, and Jamie's body crashed into the fray again.

"Jesus Christ," Jamie said. "Someone put me out of my misery."

"Not sure we can, chief." Freon sounded philosophical. "Froze you in place for now."

"GRACIE!" Jay yelled.

Gracie ducked out of instinct, shield up, as purple fire flowed directly at her. She had triggered all of her blocking abilities, and they were eaten up within a split second.

This fire was *insanely* powerful.

A backstab and poison left Harry's character stunned, and their resident rogue, Xin, gave a little laugh. "Don't try to out-cheat a rogue, idiot." He melted back into stealth as Harry rounded on him.

Gracie, sensing her opportunity, took her chance and sprinted away through the oasis. Harry's shriek of rage came a second too late, and she threw herself around the edge of the doorway as more purple flame shot through it.

"Shit." She was panting. She got her character upright and kept running down the hallway. She didn't want to say anything lest she let on to Harry that the team was here, so she would have to hope they were paying attention.

"You think you can block every hit?" Harry called furiously.

Fire exploded through the enclosed space.

"No, but we can sure as hell blind *you*," Ushanas said, her tone deeply satisfied. "Dathok?"

Dathok had respecced to a sender, and now he enfolded Harry in a dark magic spell. It wouldn't work, of course, if Harry was now a demon. Demons weren't vulnerable to dark magic.

But the point wasn't damage, it was to obscure Harry's view. As his character twisted and shrieked its rage, Gracie skittered up the toppled column and onto the roof. Harry had focused on the oasis with his team, so she would bet that he hadn't explored the possibilities this map had to offer.

She was up on the roof in time to see Harry fly down the corridor at high speed, breathing flames at everyone.

"Don't give him more bodies to work with," Gracie reminded the team in an undertone.

"Roger that," Freon said. "We're all in position, boss."

"Don't call me that. It's weird."

"Aye aye, Captain."

"I swear to God, I will kill you 'til you die from it." Gracie crept forward along the roof. "Give me a countdown when he's close."

"Not quite yet," Jamie said. "He's wandering around. I'm following like an undead puppy and slashing at things. It's...disconcerting."

"Shhh." Gracie laughed.

"Oh, right. *YO, HARRY. ASSFACE. I'M A ZOMBIE, LALALALALALALA—*"

"Everyone else mute Jamie?" Gracie asked.

"Yep," Alan said. "Bless his little zombie heart."

"He's coming your way," Lakhesis reported. "Five... four...three—"

"Mages, go," Ushanas reported.

"Two...*one.*"

Gracie leapt from the roof as Harry soared underneath, bringing her axe down in her biggest stunning strike. A gigantic spear of ice sprouted through Harry's chest, Xin appeared for a flurry of strikes and poisons, and Jay sliced at Harry's legs to create a bleed effect. His health bar plunged, and Gracie and Lakhesis traded stunning strikes as everyone piled on. Harry threw one last spell, but it was a near miss, only taking Gracie's health bar down to half.

His character twisted in mid-air as the demonic possession left it and flopped to the ground, and Gracie felt a surge of happiness.

"*YES!*"

CHALLENGE STARTED flashed across the screen.

"Wait, what?"

She was still looking around when Thad's ultimate strike took her sideways and sent her skidding across the floor, haptics shuddering. Her health bar was at twenty percent as he advanced on her.

"Oh, you have *got* to be kidding me," Gracie exclaimed.

"Gracie." Alan's voice was panicked. "I'm trying to heal you and I can't. Nothing's happening. Gracie?"

"Solo challenge." Gracie scrambled back. "It has to be. That must have been one of the options. Son of a *bitch.*"

And all of her cooldowns had been used up on Harry's fire. They would be coming back up in about a minute, but that was a long time in a duel.

She faced Thad down and narrowed her eyes. "I knew there was another reason you hadn't left yet."

"How does it feel?" Thad's tone was tight. He feinted left, then followed her when she dodged right, slamming his shield against hers. His character's face was almost more frightening given its utter blankness. "To know you're outmatched, to know your opponent has an impossible advantage?"

"Tell me one goddamned time you knew that," Gracie spat back. Rather than back away, she threw a stun at him and a heavy blow with her axe, then slid into the darkness. Her team scattered behind her. "You went into the last Month First with inside information and your own gear. You have all your expenses paid for you. You train in a high-end facility. Tell me you *ever* went into a matchup with me where you didn't have the advantage." Fury was making her breath come short. "Like right now—waiting until I was almost dead and then striking."

Something cold resolved in her chest. She was *not* going to die here. Not like this.

Not to Thad.

Like hell would *he* take this from her.

Across the hallway, she saw Jamie give her a nod. He didn't say anything. He didn't need to.

Gracie began to dance. She rushed Thad and slid sideways at the last moment. She kited him. She ducked under his swings and stunned him when he tried to follow her. She was always moving, never still, never in range. It was intense, and she was already coated with sweat, but she shoved that to the back of her mind.

Who you are is best defined by what you do when you think you have nothing left.

Thad, driven to react rather than push his offensive, began to lose his temper. He got her once, a strike that took hit points she didn't have to lose, but he wasn't as fast as she was, and he wasn't as used to fighting without a team.

Gracie had done this before. He hadn't.

"You know how this ends," Gracie said. "Cancel the challenge, and you get to stay in the game. Keep going, and you'll be gone forever."

"Oh, I'm not losing this one." Thad's tone was triumphant. "You know time's up for you, and you're trying to bargain. There's nothing you can offer me."

"I'm not trying to bargain," Gracie said. She slashed at

him, attacked, and—when he waited for her to slide away—kept the attack going with a shield bash. "I'm trying to save something that's important to you. What quarrel do we really have with one another?"

Other than the fact that he was a douche canoe, of course.

"You made me look like a fool," Thad hissed. He had recovered from the shield bash, and he threw his shield at her but missed. He was so assured of his win that he didn't seem to care.

"If you wanted to play a competition-based game without ever losing, you set yourself up for failure," Gracie informed him. "Everyone loses sometimes."

"Like you. Right now." Thad attacked with a feral smile.

But Gracie's cooldowns were back up. She sank into a crouch, each hit giving her health as her first timer counted down. Then the time was up and she set her other two in motion, increasing her block chance and absorbing damage. She went on the offensive, hitting with her shield, blocking his strikes with her axe, ducking out of the way, and dancing back in for a strike.

She didn't have to fight the whole battle right now, after all. She just had to be a little better in this one encounter—a little faster, a little stronger. She just had to come out of this encounter better off, and the next one, and the next one. She had to trust her instincts to keep her away from the traps he was trying to maneuver her into. As long as it took, she would do it. She wouldn't throw her entire time in this game away for one useless strike.

And the tide began to turn.

How long it took for Thad to realize it, she didn't know,

but he began to get sloppier. He was running, backing away down the hallway. It was sinking in, the truth of what he'd done.

And the possibility of failure.

"Cancel. The challenge." Gracie followed him, her ultimate flashing to let her know it was ready. "You can still walk away from this. Cancel it."

"Fuck. You," Thad spat back. "Fuck you, you self-important bitch."

Gracie yelled her anger. She didn't want to be the person who banned him, so she didn't.

But she couldn't cancel it, she could only concede, and like hell was she going to do that.

He was the one who'd made it zero-sum, not her.

She unleashed her ultimate and watched as his body thudded to the ground.

Cheers came to her ears, and she turned to look at the rest of them.

"The others?" she asked.

"Not willing to die for Thad," Jamie said. "They all logged out."

Several top-tier heals hit her the next second, and Jamie and Alan said in unison, "Just in case."

Gracie laughed, then the shaking started. She stared down at Thad's body and felt her chin trembling, then her gaze went to Harry's body, small and still.

"It's done," Alex said from her shoulder. She leaned against him, then realized he must have come up to her in the real world as well. They all had; her entire team crowded around her, and Gracie broke down as they held her up. Some of them had glitched out of their VR areas and their characters were shimmering in midair, but she felt them join the giant group hug.

It was over. It didn't seem real, but it was over.

The game could finally face a new dawn.

Finally, she pulled away and wiped her face. "You know the ridiculous thing?"

"What?" Jay took her hand, both in the real world and in *Metamorphosis*.

"No one knows," Gracie said. "Almost no one has any idea this happened."

"I've always thought that's how most of the great battles are fought," Ushanas said. "A small group risking everything, and everyone else blissfully unaware. Makes you wonder how often it happens."

Gracie looked around herself. "So, what do we do now?"

Someone cleared their throat, and they looked around to see Yaro standing there. His bow was very courtly.

"Might I suggest you get some sleep?"

They all exchanged looks.

"And then we have a party," Dhruv said. "Obviously."

CHAPTER TWENTY-NINE

When Gracie woke up the next morning, Jay was snoring gently on the bed, one arm flung out. They had gotten back to the hotel too tired to do anything except stare at the ceiling and fall almost instantly into a deep sleep.

Judging by the state of things, she had forgotten to brush her teeth.

She took a long shower, brushed her teeth more than once, and came out to find Jay still dead to the world. Her stomach, however, was anything but dead, and it informed her that it wanted to be fed *now*.

When she got downstairs, only Jamie was there. Gracie paused at the edge of the buffet area and watching him push eggs around on his plate. Finally, she gave up trying to divine what it was and walked over. He jumped when she pulled out a chair and sat, and gave her a vaguely hunted look.

"Do you want to talk about it?" Gracie asked him. "Or is that the last thing you want to do?"

He swallowed. "I did something dumb."

She frowned. "Look, if this is about what you told Thad, I get why you did it. I'm not mad. Harry was cheating, and Thad certainly took advantage. If you fight people like that head-on, you get steamrolled, and then they take over."

"Not that." Jamie sounded almost sick. He leaned his head into his hands. "Oh, God."

Now Gracie was actually concerned. She leaned forward and reached out to touch his arm lightly. "Jamie? Are you *okay?* Is something wrong?"

He started to laugh while shaking his head. "It's stupid, and it's nothing important, I'm just… I don't know how to deal."

"Okay." Gracie made a decision. "How about this? I'll go get some food, you figure out if you want to talk about it *right now*, and if you don't, we'll just have a lazy breakfast and then go for a walk or something."

He gave her a grateful smile and nodded wordlessly.

At the buffet, she piled her plate with eggs and bacon and chowed down on a yogurt while her bagel toasted. Armed with all the fixings for an epic breakfast sandwich, she headed back to the table and began assembling it, assiduously not looking at Jamie while she did so.

She was just trying to figure out how to take a bite of the damned thing when he blurted, "I think I'm in love."

Gracie put the sandwich down. "That's so sweet!"

"No!" Jamie looked panicked. "It's not!"

Gracie blinked as she tried to parse this. "Uh…is she underage?" she asked delicately. "Oh, God. She's human, right? Tell me she's not a pillow."

Jamie sank his head into one hand. "She's not a *pillow*."

At the raised eyebrow, he threw up his hands. "She's not underage, either, Jesus. She's also..." Gracie made a faint anxious sound, "not a *she*."

It took Gracie way longer than it should have to put it together. "Huh," she said and picked up her egg sandwich again. "I mean, I'm sorry. I guess I just assumed you were straight." She took a bite, mostly for something to do.

"So did I," Jamie said in a very small voice.

That was when it clicked. Gracie choked on her sandwich, dropped it, and stared at him with a mouthful of egg and sausage. "*Ke-then?*"

"Shut *up*," Jamie hissed, looked around desperately, as though he would be found out. He waved his hand. "Don't tell anyone. Oh, God."

Gracie clapped a hand over her mouth as she stared at him. It all made sense now—the way he would laugh and joke and get so invested in the conversation, then look totally blindsided and unsure of himself. The way he hadn't wanted to tell anyone what was going on.

"Oh," she said finally. She took his hand. "How are you doing?"

"Not great," Jamie said. "My parents are gonna lose their shit. I mean, probably not. I just... A lot of stuff makes sense right now that I kind of wish didn't? And, like...oh, God." He dropped his head onto his arms. "He's perfect," he said, his voice muffled. "You've seen him now. He's *perfect*. He has everything."

"Does he?" Gracie asked gently. "Because I don't think he's dating anyone, and I know he's trying, so it's not like he *wants* to be single. And he talks a lot of shit about being a disappointment to his parents, but from my own experience, that's the sort of thing that isn't exactly *easy*. And…" She weighed whether to say this, then shrugged and gave up. "You've seen how he looks at you, right?"

Jamie's head came up. "Really?"

"Really," Gracie said. She hunched her shoulders. "If you want my take, I'd say he would never make a move while you were staying with him because he'd feel like it was creepy. You know, you didn't realize you were gay—or bi, or whatever—and you didn't have anywhere else to go. But you make him laugh. He's been happier in the past couple of weeks than I've seen him before."

She let go of his hand and took another bite, looking away to let him process this in relative privacy.

"I'm still kind of shell-shocked," Jamie said finally. "Is there a word for when you just always assumed you were one thing and then you realized you weren't, and all of a sudden a lot of dots start connecting?"

Gracie gave him a commiserating look. "There definitely should be." She sighed. "Look, this is more complicated than Jay and me. I get that. I think it's always terrifying to tell someone you're into them."

"I feel like I shouldn't tell him," Jamie said in a small voice. "Until I know…*what* I am."

"Hot take," Gracie said, putting her sandwich down. "Does it matter?"

Jamie stared at her.

"Okay, you've now mixed those eggs and ketchup into a *paste* and it's really grossing me out." She put a napkin over his plate. "Where was I? Right. Look, you know you like Kevin, right?"

Jamie looked faintly like a deer in the headlights but he nodded.

"Maybe that's all you need to figure out right now," Gracie said and shrugged. "As long as you're honest with him..."

Jamie had stopped paying attention. He was looking across the room to where Kevin had just emerged from the elevator bank and now looked a bit queasy.

"Should I go?" Gracie asked delicately. "Or would you rather I stay?"

"I don't know yet," Jamie said, looking at her with mute appeal.

Gracie smiled and took a sip of her coffee.

It was going to be an interesting few days.

That day was a lazy affair, punctuated by people slithering out of bed at intervals, lying next to the pool, and winding up draped over the couches in the main suite. Chowder straight-up bought a coffee maker for the group, along with several boxes of pastries, and people lay around talking, laughing, and—in Jamie's case—studiously not looking at Kevin.

Gracie tried to keep from looking at Jamie. If she did, she knew her face would be a picture, and then she'd have to explain it to Jay, and she wanted to give Jamie time to figure it out for himself.

"Well," Chowder said, sometime around dinner, "what do you all say I get some pizzas and we bring that tequila out again?"

There were some cheers.

"I'd wait a few moments on the alcohol," said a new voice. Everyone turned to see Dan and Dhruv, as well as Sam.

Gracie felt exhausted suddenly. This had been such a good day, not worrying about the game, but now she was worried all over again.

"We have an offer to make," Dan said, "and I think it would be best if we at least *presented* it while you were all sober."

Gracie looked at Jay, who shrugged. Whatever this was, he didn't know about it. She looked back and found the rest of the team staring at her, so she nodded to Dan and Dhruv.

"All right."

Dan came to lean against the window, apparently unconcerned about the steep drop behind him. "Very well. As I think you all know by now, Gracie's quest was created without our knowledge and has boosted her ranking in ways we cannot control. We believe that she, however, can."

Gracie swallowed. She wasn't sure she liked where this was going.

Dhruv picked up. "One of our main mechanics in the game is that we pay the people in the top-ranked spots. Everyone in Red Squadron has experienced a boost that they otherwise would not have had. While this is technically a game mechanic, it is also something most players do not have access to."

Gracie folded her hands in her lap. Jay's eyes were narrowed, and Alex was chewing on his lip.

"We would like to make an exchange," Dan said finally. He had his businessman smile on, which didn't necessarily make things better. "Right now, you receive considerable compensation for your rankings. We would like to increase that by offering you employment at Dragon Soul."

"You would still have a place in the game," Dhruv said, "but not in the rankings. Like our other GMs, you would resolve player problems and give us feedback on how the game might be improved."

"We've researched." Dan looked around at all of them. "If you don't want to be GMs, all of you have skills we can use as Dragon Soul expands. We need accountants, software developers, department coordinators..." He waved his hands. "Relocation costs could be negotiated as necessary."

"Why are you offering this?" Gracie asked bluntly. To her surprise, tears were stinging her eyes, although she didn't know why. She was almost angry.

Dan took his time before answering. "We have heard a lot recently," he said finally, "about fairness." He gave Jay a wry smile. "And about people loving the game, and doing what they did because they wanted to protect it. We have to look out for what's best for *all* of our players, and having a bug in the rankings isn't best for them. But we've seen how much every one of you cares—for each other and for the game. Gracie spoke to us about what the game meant to all of you, which is something we had lost sight of over the years."

"We could use you on the team." Dhruv didn't have a way with words, Gracie reflected, but he was very to the point, and there were worse things. "We knew Gracie would never agree to take you all out of the rankings unless you got something in return." He smiled at all of them, and then at Gracie. "So we thought about what she would want for her team."

Gracie swallowed hard. "That's nice, but it's not just my call."

"Proposal," Chowder said. "We have a few days to decide. All of us. One way or another." He looked around at people. "I know I wouldn't mind heading out here. I don't have much going on in San Fran."

Alex looked at Sydney, and Gracie's heart squeezed.

"Chowder has a good idea," she said to everyone. "And not everyone would have to relocate, either, even if they took the offer—right?"

"Right." Dan nodded.

"We'll think about it," Gracie said.

Both men hesitated, then nodded and left quietly.

In the silence that followed, everyone looked around. Gracie crossed her arms over her chest.

"Jay? You're the only one who actually works there."

"Drinks first," Lakhesis interrupted, "decisions later."

"Nope," Gracie said, uncompromising. "Facts, *then* drinking, *then* decisions. Well…drinking, then hangovers, then recovery, *then* decisions."

"I'll be around to answer specific questions," Jay said, "but I think you should consider it. It's a pretty good team."

"Anything else we should all think about?" Gracie asked. When everyone looked at her blankly, she laughed. "Okay, it's a big decision. Chowder's right: let's hang out and decompress, and we'll take some time to decide. Chowder, pop that bottle."

Chowder climbed over the couch and got the tequila out, grabbing shot glasses and lining them up on the table.

Gracie snagged the first one but didn't drink. Instead, with everyone focused on Chowder, she brought the glass over to Jamie.

"Liquid courage?" she asked.

He smiled at her. "I, uh…I think I'm going to try to talk about this sober."

"Probably wiser." Gracie took the shot before he thought better of it. "I'd do it now if you want both of you to be sober…unless you want to wait. But you look like you're about to jump right out of your skin, man."

Jamie looked like he wanted to cry. "Yeah."

"Talk to him," Gracie advised. She circled back around to where Jay was standing and met his curious gaze blandly. "So, we might be coworkers."

"Yeah, yeah." He looked at Jamie. "You figured out what was up with him?"

Gracie purposely didn't look at him, but she knew where Jamie was looking—and she knew, because she had paid attention, that Kevin was studiously trying not to look back. She had observed that he always seemed to know exactly where Jamie was in the room.

"I think you'll know soon," she said with a smile, "but it's about the cutest thing ever." She sighed and leaned her head on his shoulder.

"Proposal," Jay said.

"Hmm?"

"How about we have a proper date?" He looked down at her. "I know everyone's talking and hanging out and so on, but we'll be seeing them a lot for the next few days. How about we go have a real date?"

Gracie smiled up at him, then sobered. "I don't know. My last date was a shitshow."

Jay gave a laugh. "Wait 'til you hear about mine."

"Okay." Gracie grinned. "Let's go."

AUTHOR NOTES - NATALIE GREY

MAY 7, 2019

Thank you so much for reading Metamorphosis Online!

When Michael and I first began speaking about this series, we didn't know how long it would go. We batted around several ideas, and so it was a big surprise to us to sit down after this last book and say, "I think this was meant to be a trilogy." Neither of us are people who like to leave our characters, and we *definitely* don't want to leave the world of Metamorphosis Online - but this trilogy really does stand alone, and we wanted to let it do that.

There is a lot coming up with some other characters, and fairly soon you'll be hearing about some other authors joining this world, which will be *awesome.* Stay tuned!

With that said, I do have a fairly big announcement: I will be stepping back into the realm of having a day job for a while. I have enjoyed the heck out of writing full time, but when an organization nearby reached out about a role they'd been having trouble filling, I realized how much I had missed using some of my other skills.

I am not going to stop writing—frankly, I can't imagine

a world where I'm not writing! However, I won't be able to get books to you all as fast, and I thought you should know why. I am excited for this change, and excited to keep being a part of the LMBPN team. There is a lot coming up that I'll be working on: a side project related to Metamorphosis, more *Dragon Corps,* and an epic fantasy series that's been in the works for a while!

Until next time,
Nat

AUTHOR NOTES - MICHAEL ANDERLE

MAY 8, 2019

THANK YOU for not only reading this story but these *Author Notes* as well.

(I think I've been good with always opening with "thank you." If not, I need to edit the other *Author Notes*!)

RANDOM (*sometimes*) THOUGHTS?

I've collaborated with Nat since 2016.

We have worked off and on during that time as she worked with others, on her own books, and with me and LMBPN. This series (in my opinion) has been the one where we both dug deep to really figure out what it was like to work on something we BOTH had strong feelings about.

And I'm seriously proud that I have my name on this book.

Natalie is a gamer, she has the cred - she has done the time and has the marks to prove it. Many of them emotional.

When I collaborate, I have a blast pulling interesting

facts from my collaborators and placing those aspects into our characters. However, there was an aspect of being emotionally mistreated while playing tabletop D&D that neither of us wanted to ignore. We struggled to find a point where we were both happy with how we presented the hurt and joy that online multiplayer games can bring to individuals.

I'm pleased with the result and the way we portrayed the BETTER side of gaming. The part(s) that don't make headlines, and where people don't give a flying @#%@#% if you are male or female. All they want to know is if they like playing with you.

And the funny stuff!

For example, I was telling her a story about how new guys will find a girl ('chick') avatar on games like World of Warcraft and chase them, not realizing it's just another guy playing a female character.

So, with the maturity of MMORPG's, most male players start to assume that females are just guys playing female characters.

So, wouldn't it be funny if the guys all assumed she was male?

And then, the size of the sword jokes?

Ok, I admit that was ribald humor, but I still smile about it.

I will still get to work with Natalie, but DAMN I'm going to miss the next few books as she has to slow down with her writing production.

THANK YOU NAT for sticking with us through this wonderful change in your life.

(See you next week... somewhere.)

AROUND THE WORLD IN 80 DAYS

One of the interesting (at least to me) aspects of my life is the ability to work from anywhere and at any time. In the future, I hope to re-read my own *Author Notes* and remember my life as a diary entry.

Cave in the Sky (™) Las Vegas, NV USA

It's just about midnight as I type these notes. I feared it would take a while but mentioning just a little about Natalie was easy-peasy. I decided not to keep chatting, because I could type another 2,000 words on our professional career.

During the time I've known her, she and her husband have moved, had a child, lived through the early childhood stages, and I've just shaken my head at their nickname for their son.

Sprog.

I saw him a few days ago as Natalie shared the good news as he walked around getting into all sorts of stuff.

I bet the next time I see him on video, he will be telling her how to write and that she should use his crayon.

I hope I remember to record that.

FAN PRICING

$0.99 Saturdays (new LMBPN stuff) and $0.99 Wednesday (both LMBPN books and friends of LMBPN books.) Get great stuff from us and others at tantalizing prices.

Go ahead, I bet you can't read just one.

Sign up here: http://lmbpn.com/email/.

HOW TO MARKET FOR BOOKS YOU LOVE

Review them so others have your thoughts, tell friends and the dogs of your enemies (because who wants to talk with enemies?)… *Enough said ;-)*

Ad Aeternitatem,

Michael Anderle

BOOKS BY NATALIE GREY

Shadows of Magic

Bound Sorcery

Blood Sorcery

Bright Sorcery

Set in the Kurtherian Gambit Universe

Bellatrix

Challenges

Risk Be Damned

Damned to Hell

Vigilante

Sentinel

Warden

Paladin

Justiciar

Defender

Protector

Writing as Moira Katson

Shadowborn

Shadowforged

Shadow's End

Daughter of Ashes

Mahalia

BOOKS BY MICHAEL ANDERLE

For a complete list of books by Michael Anderle, please visit

www.lmbpn.com/ma-books/

All LMBPN Audiobooks are Available at Audible.com and iTunes. For a complete list of audiobooks visit:

www.lmbpn.com/audible

CONNECT WITH THE AUTHORS

Natalie Grey Social

Email List

https://landing.mailerlite.com/webforms/landing/w0k9j4

Follow Natalie on Amazon

https://www.amazon.com/Natalie-Grey/e/B01MYG7K8P/

Facebook

https://www.facebook.com/Natalie-Grey-393234677682987/

Michael Anderle Social

Website: http://lmbpn.com

Email List: http://lmbpn.com/email/

Facebook:
www.facebook.com/TheKurtherianGambitBooks

Made in the USA
Lexington, KY
17 June 2019